SUPER KING VIKING LAND!

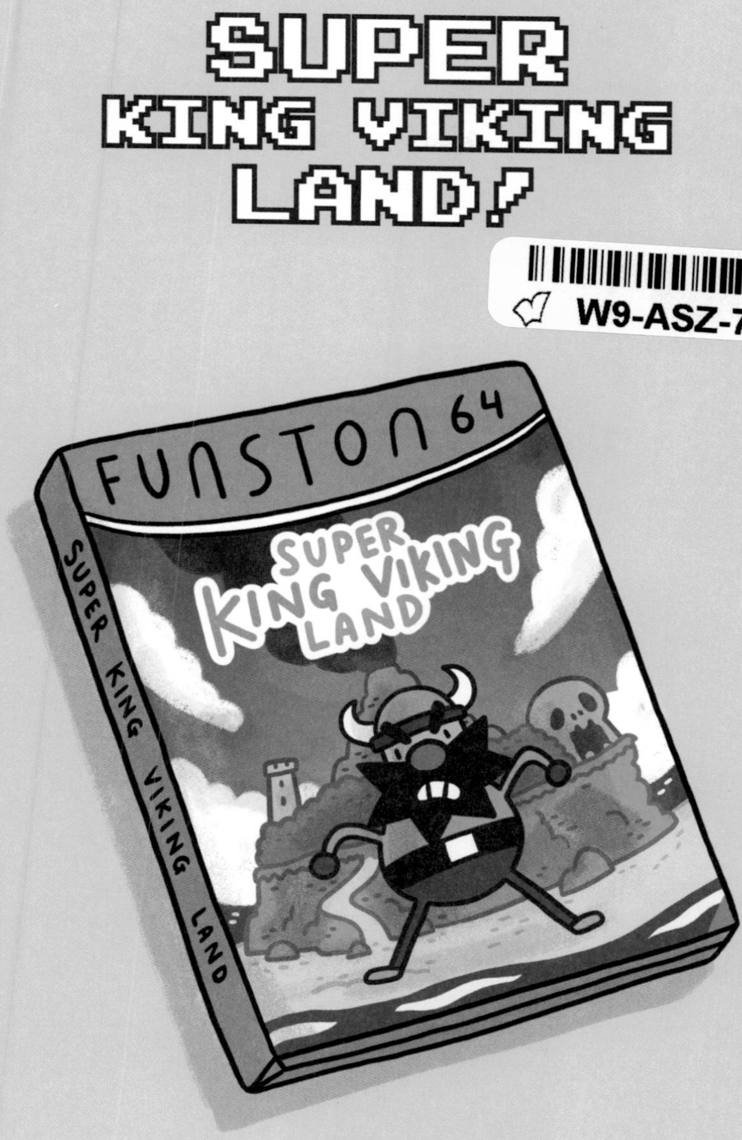
FUNSTON 64
SUPER KING VIKING LAND
SUPER KING VIKING LAND

READ MORE PRESS START! BOOKS!

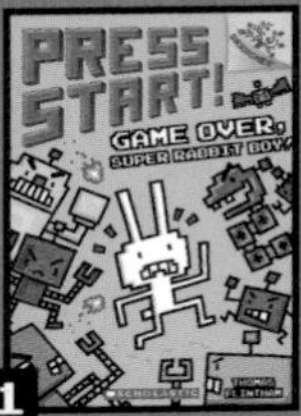
PRESS START!
GAME OVER, SUPER RABBIT BOY!
SCHOLASTIC
THOMAS FLINTHAM
1

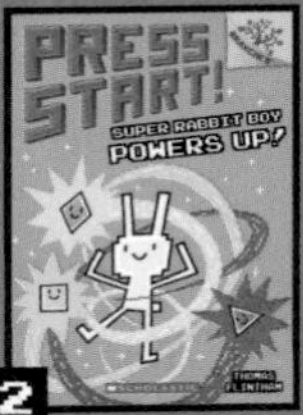
PRESS START!
SUPER RABBIT BOY POWERS UP!
SCHOLASTIC
THOMAS FLINTHAM
2

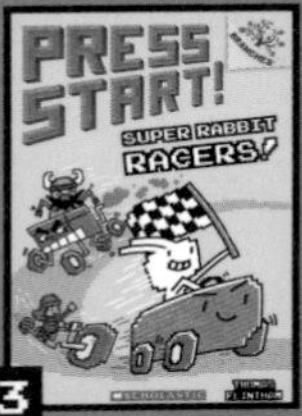
PRESS START!
SUPER RABBIT RACERS!
SCHOLASTIC
THOMAS FLINTHAM
3

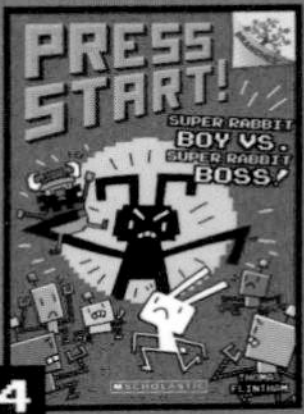
PRESS START!
SUPER RABBIT BOY VS. SUPER RABBIT BOSS!
SCHOLASTIC
THOMAS FLINTHAM
4

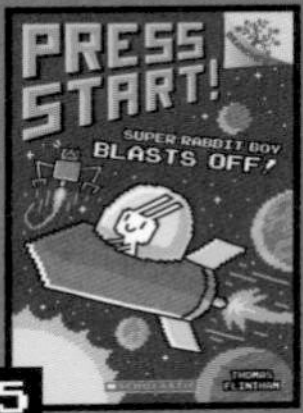
PRESS START!
SUPER RABBIT BOY BLASTS OFF!
SCHOLASTIC
THOMAS FLINTHAM
5

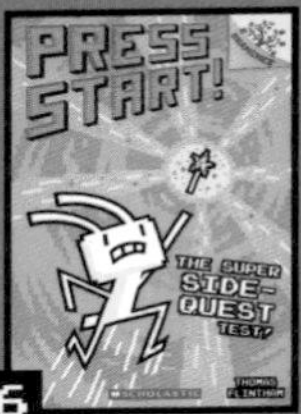
PRESS START!
THE SUPER SIDE-QUEST TEST!
SCHOLASTIC
THOMAS FLINTHAM
6

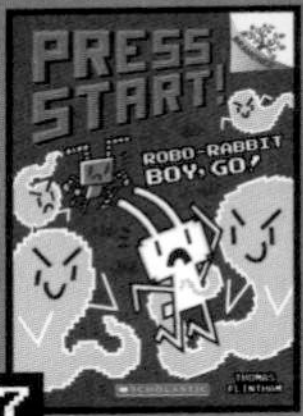
PRESS START!
ROBO-RABBIT BOY, GO!
SCHOLASTIC
THOMAS FLINTHAM
7

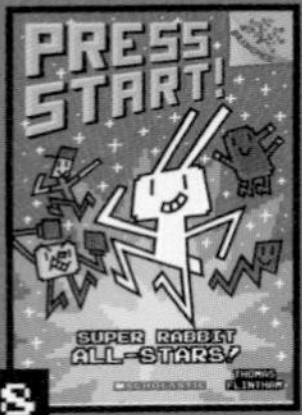
PRESS START!
SUPER RABBIT ALL-STARS!
SCHOLASTIC
THOMAS FLINTHAM
8

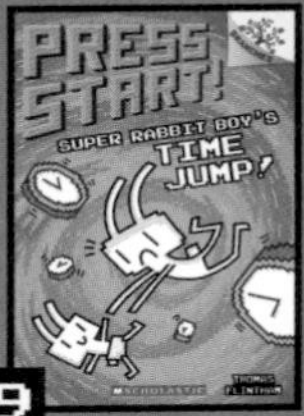
PRESS START!
SUPER RABBIT BOY'S TIME JUMP!
SCHOLASTIC
THOMAS FLINTHAM
9

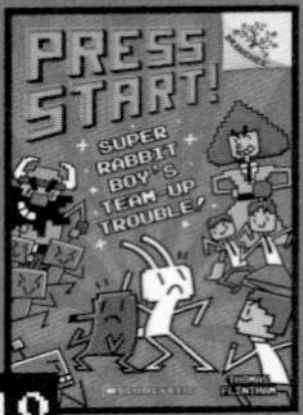
PRESS START!
SUPER RABBIT BOY'S TEAM-UP TROUBLE!
SCHOLASTIC
THOMAS FLINTHAM
10

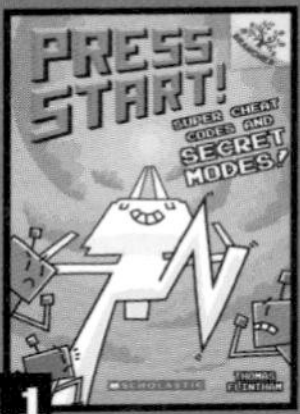
PRESS START!
SUPER CHEAT CODES AND SECRET MODES!
SCHOLASTIC
THOMAS FLINTHAM
11

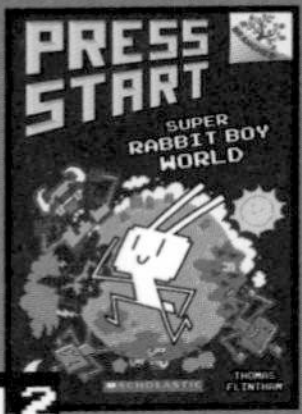
PRESS START
SUPER RABBIT BOY WORLD
SCHOLASTIC
THOMAS FLINTHAM
12

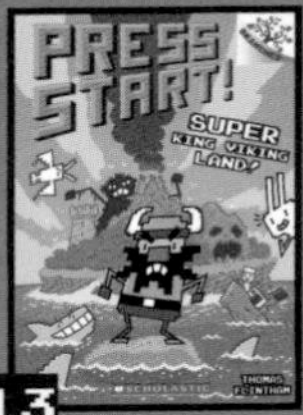
PRESS START!
SUPER KING VIKING LAND!
SCHOLASTIC
THOMAS FLINTHAM
13

MORE BOOKS COMING SOON!

PRESS START!

SUPER KING VIKING LAND!

THOMAS FLINTHAM

BRANCHES

SCHOLASTIC INC.

FOR ADAM

Copyright © 2023 by Thomas Flintham

All rights reserved. Published by Scholastic Inc., *Publishers since 1920.* SCHOLASTIC, BRANCHES, and associated logos are trademarks and/or registered trademarks of Scholastic Inc.

The publisher does not have any control over and does not assume any responsibility for author or third-party websites or their content.

No part of this publication may be reproduced, stored in a retrieval system, or transmitted in any form or by any means, electronic, mechanical, photocopying, recording, or otherwise, without written permission of the publisher. For information regarding permission, write to Scholastic Inc., Attention: Permissions Department, 557 Broadway, New York, NY 10012.

This book is a work of fiction. Names, characters, places, and incidents are either the product of the author's imagination or are used fictitiously, and any resemblance to actual persons, living or dead, business establishments, events, or locales is entirely coincidental.

Names: Flintham, Thomas, author, illustrator.
Title: Super King Viking land! / Thomas Flintham.
Description: New York: Branches/Scholastic, Inc., 2023. |
Series: Press start!; 13 | Audience: Ages 5-7. | Audience: Grades K-2. |
Summary: When Sunny's father enters a video game he finds himself as the evil King Viking, but he is not very good at playing, so King Viking finds himself falling down and getting lost, and wondering if he will ever escape from the game.
Identifiers: LCCN 2022011300 (print) | ISBN 9781338828757 (paperback) |
ISBN 9781338828764 (library binding) |
Subjects: LCSH: Superheroes—Juvenile fiction. | Supervillains—Juvenile fiction. | Video games—Juvenile fiction. | Fathers and sons—Juvenile fiction. | CYAC: Superheroes—Fiction. | Supervillains—Fiction. | Video games—Fiction. | Fathers and sons—Fiction. | LCGFT: Superhero fiction.
Classification: LCC PZ7.1.F585 So 2023 (print) |
DDC [Fic]—dc23
LC record available at https://lccn.loc.gov/2022011300

ISBN 978-1-338-82876-4 (hardcover) / ISBN 978-1-338-82875-7 (paperback)

10 9 8 7 6 5 4 3 2 1   23 24 25 26 27

Printed in China   62
First edition, April 2023
Edited by Katie Carella and Alli Brydon
Book design by Sarah Dvojack

TABLE OF CONTENTS

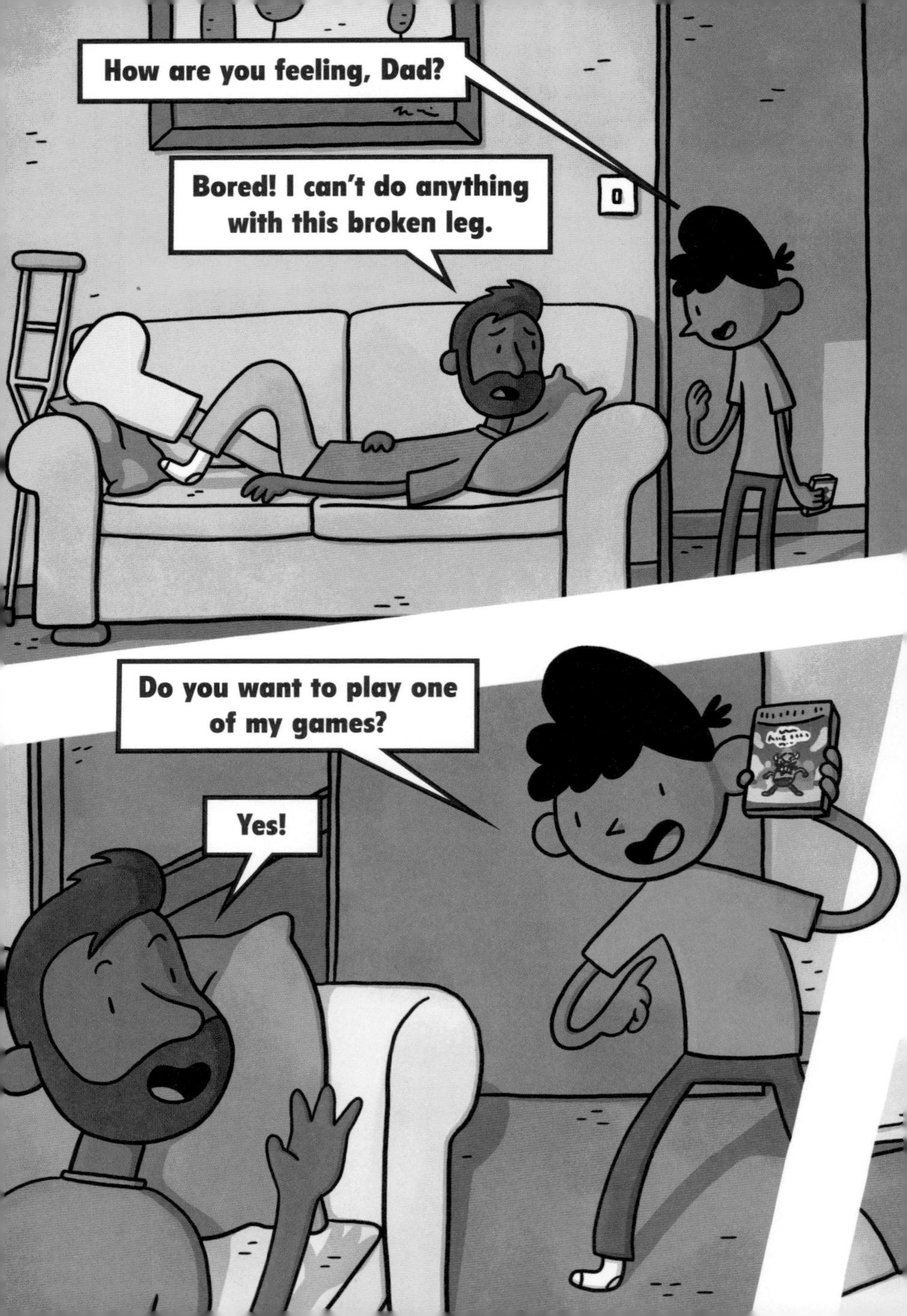
How are you feeling, Dad?
Bored! I can't do anything with this broken leg.
Do you want to play one of my games?
Yes!

1 PRESS START!

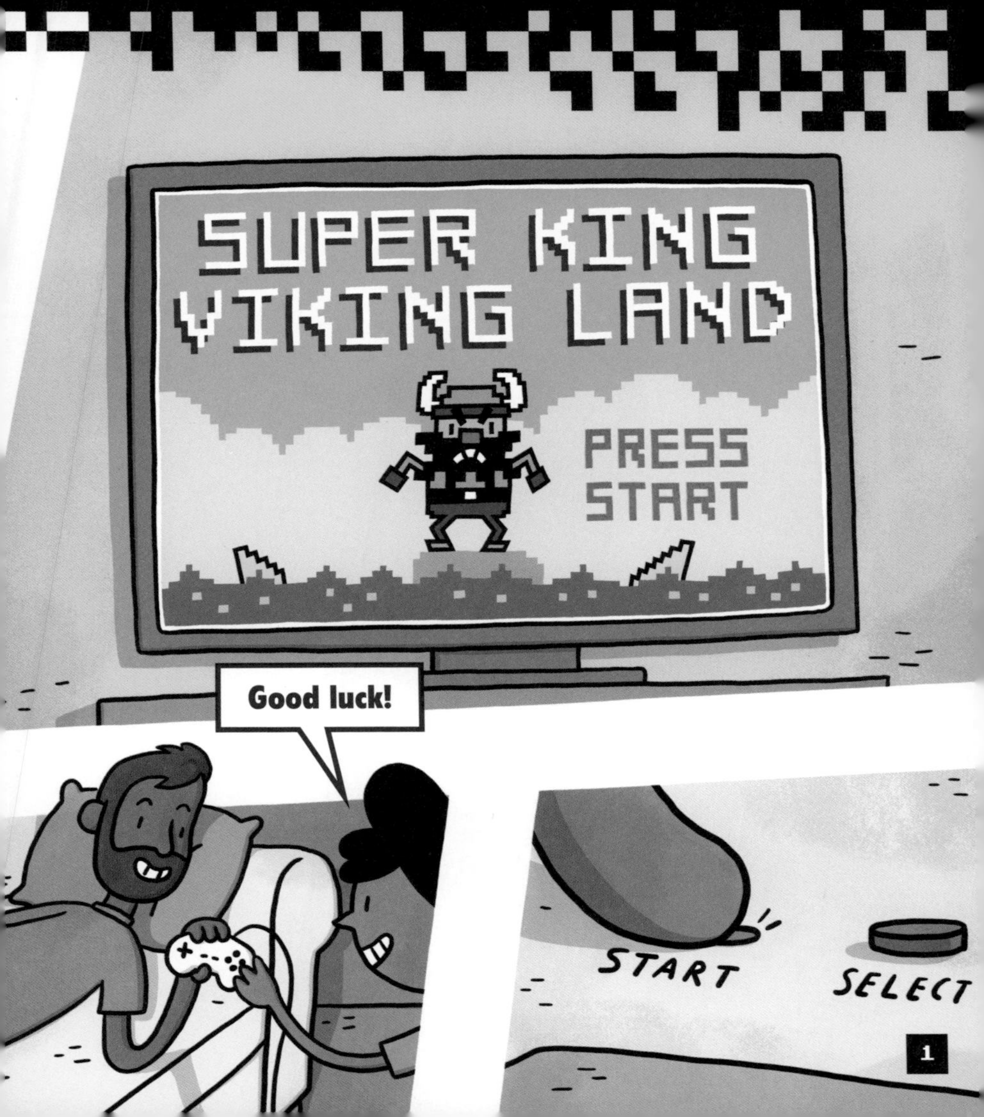
SUPER KING VIKING LAND
PRESS START
Good luck!
START
SELECT

Super Rabbit Boy and his friends are having a nice day at the beach . . . until King Viking arrives to ruin the fun!

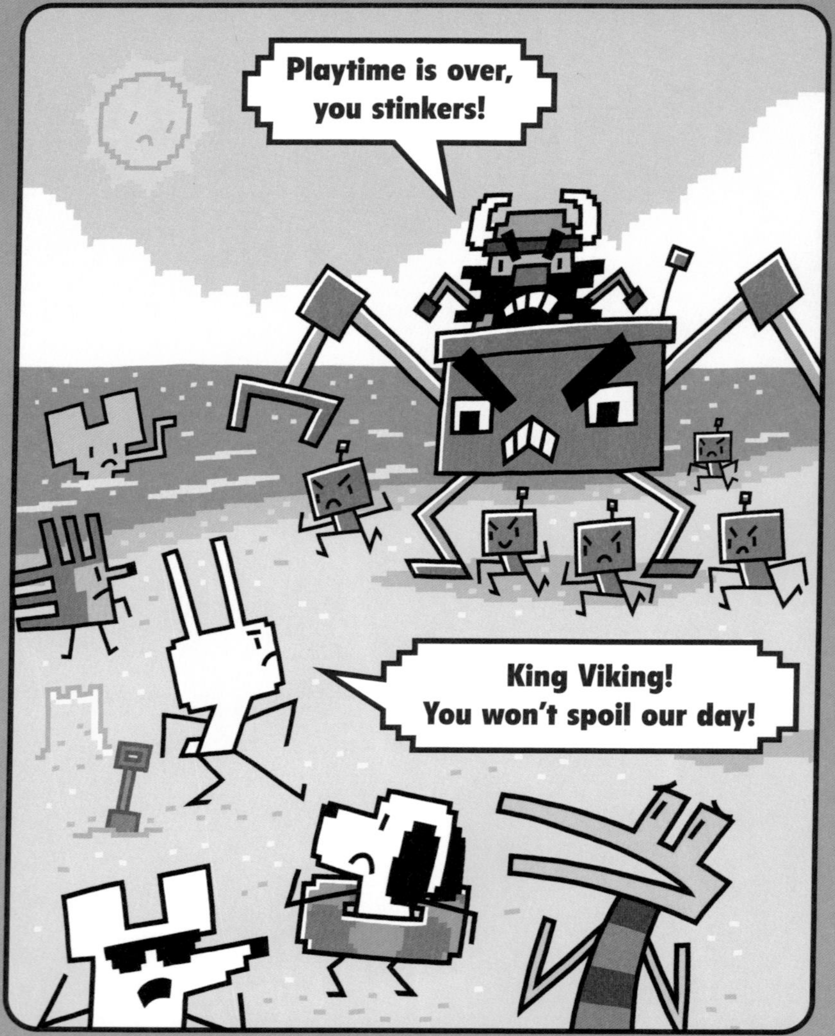
Playtime is over, you stinkers!
King Viking! You won't spoil our day!

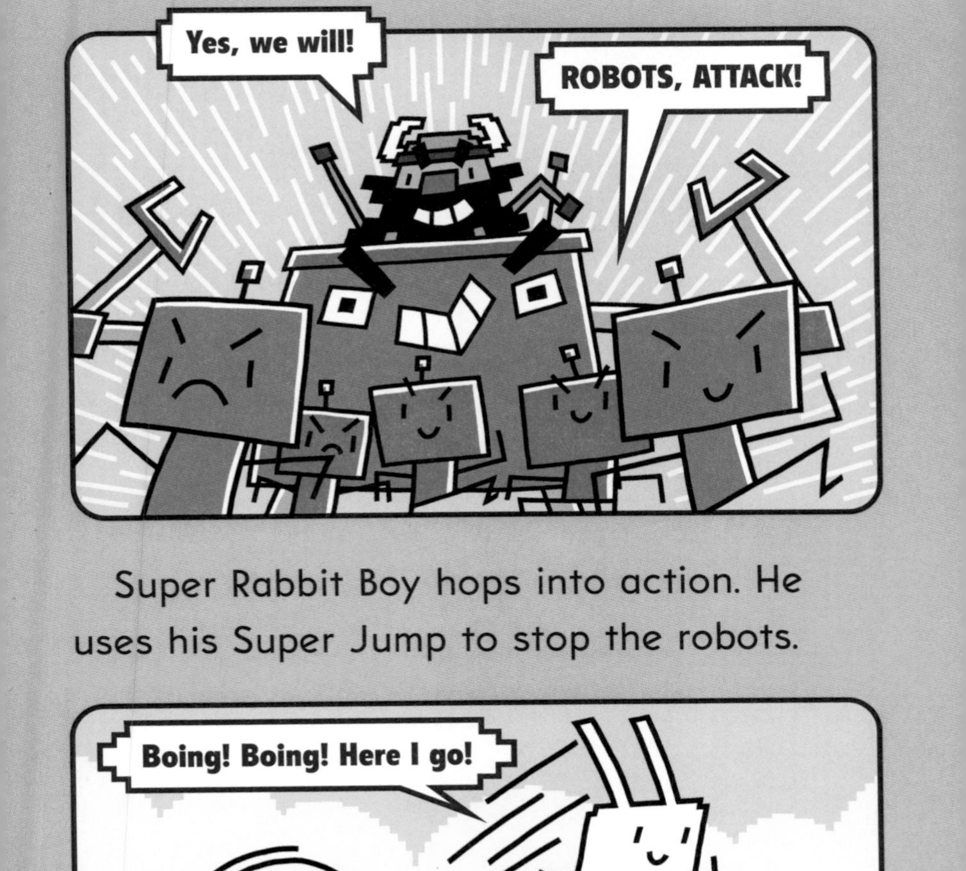
Yes, we will!
ROBOTS, ATTACK!

Super Rabbit Boy hops into action. He uses his Super Jump to stop the robots.

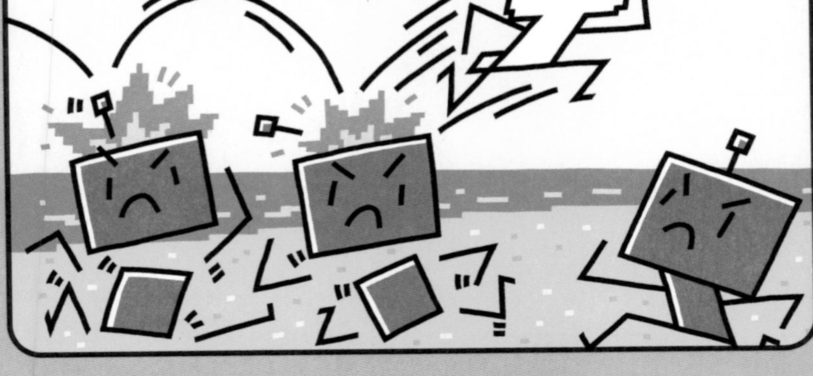
Boing! Boing! Here I go!

He defeats robot after robot.

There is just one robot left: King Viking's Robo-Boss.

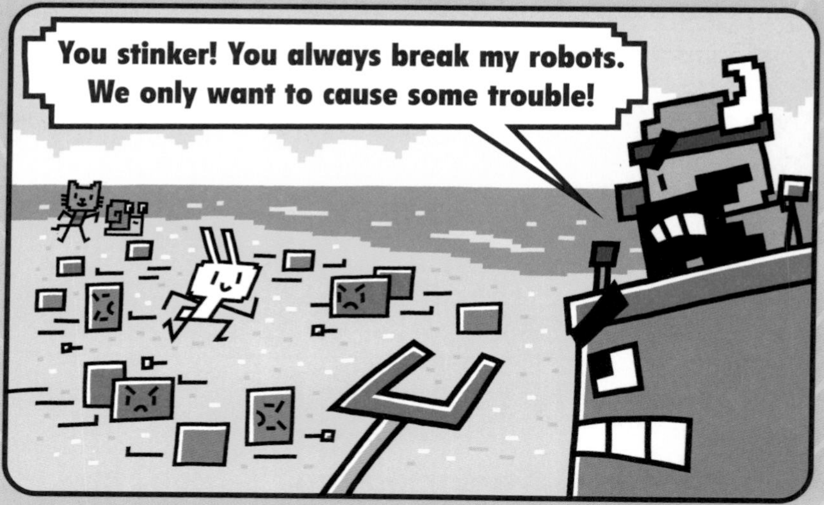
You stinker! You always break my robots. We only want to cause some trouble!

Super Rabbit Boy bounces all over the Robo-Boss. It starts to shake.

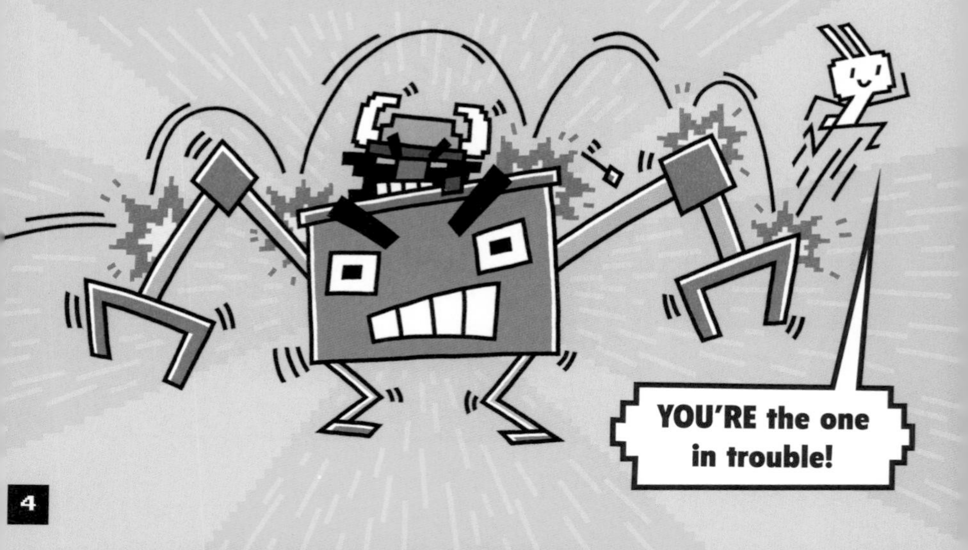
YOU'RE the one in trouble!

The Robo-Boss explodes! King Viking is sent flying into the air.

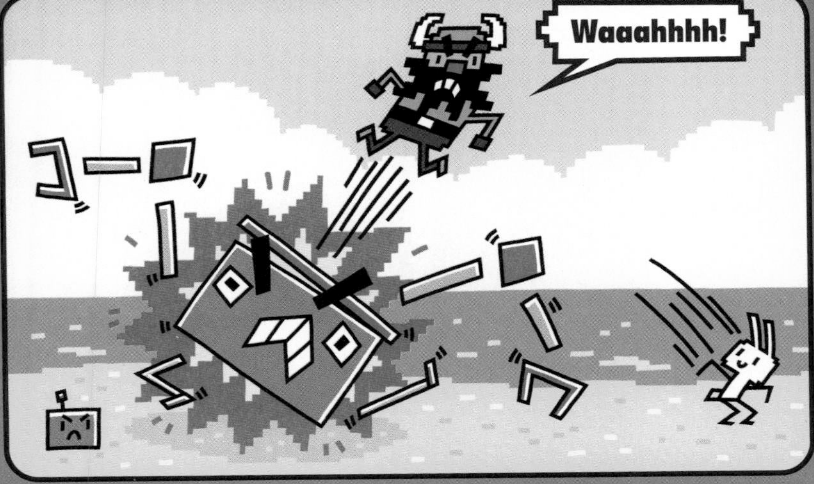
Waaahhhh!

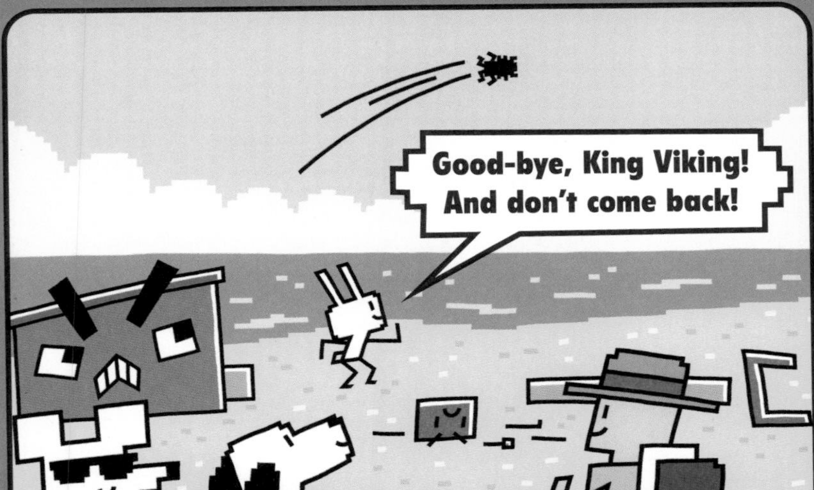
Good-bye, King Viking! And don't come back!

King Viking zooms through the sky.

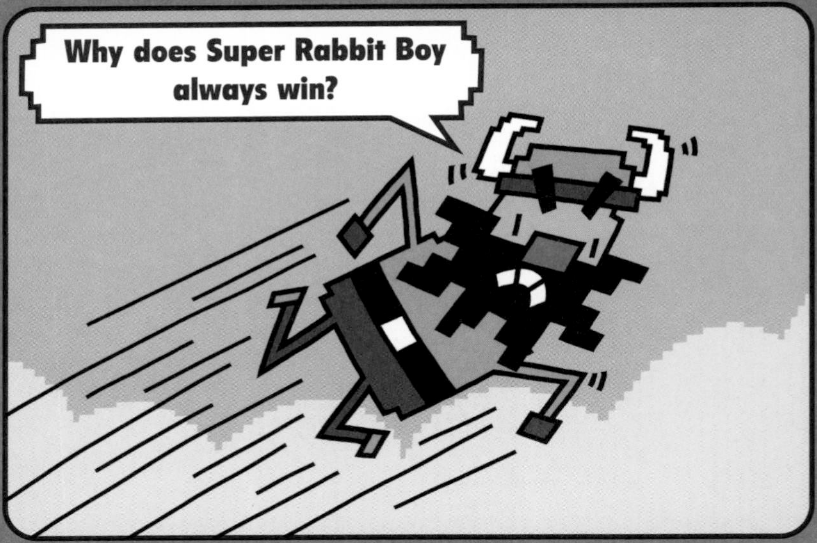
Why does Super Rabbit Boy always win?

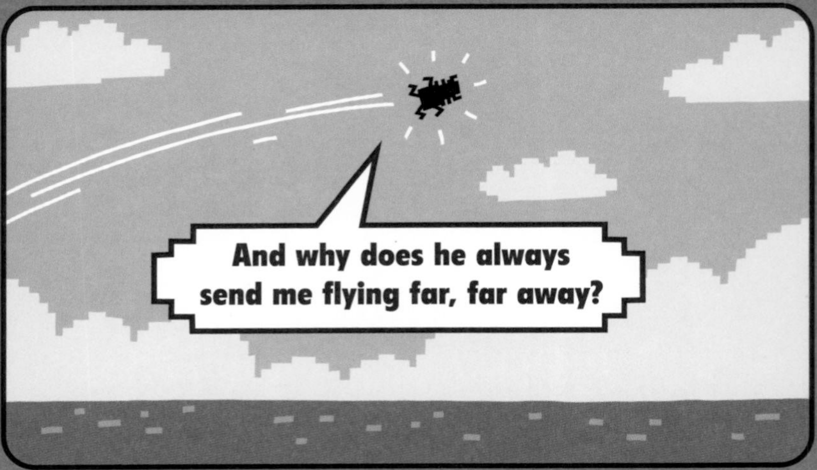
And why does he always send me flying far, far away?

King Viking falls toward a small island.

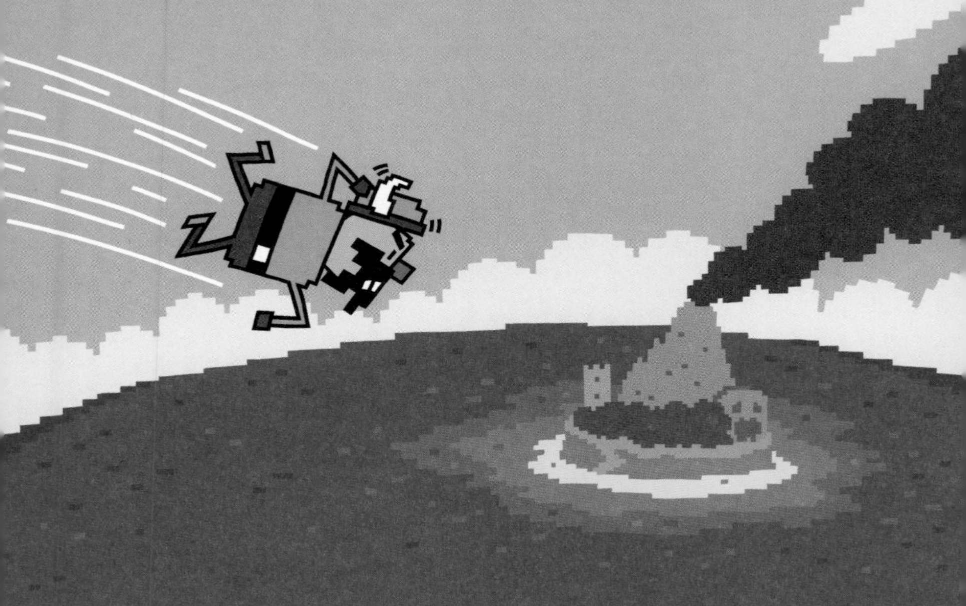

He lands on the beach with a CRASH!

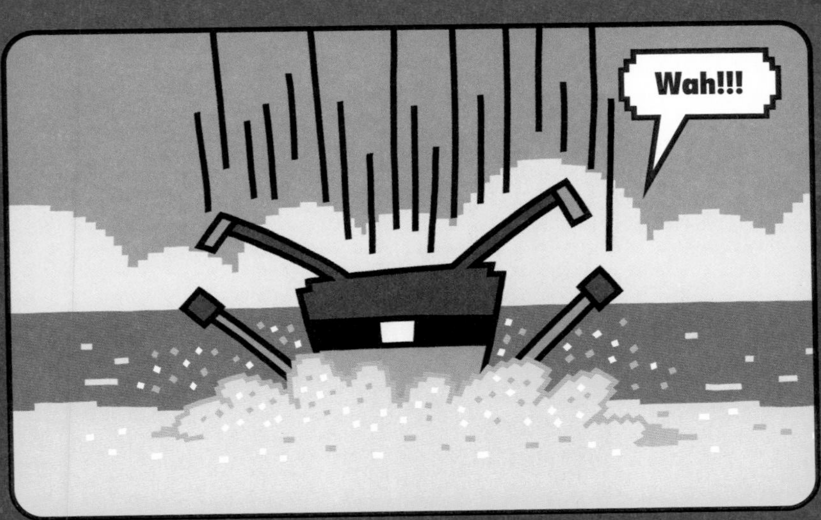
Wah!!!

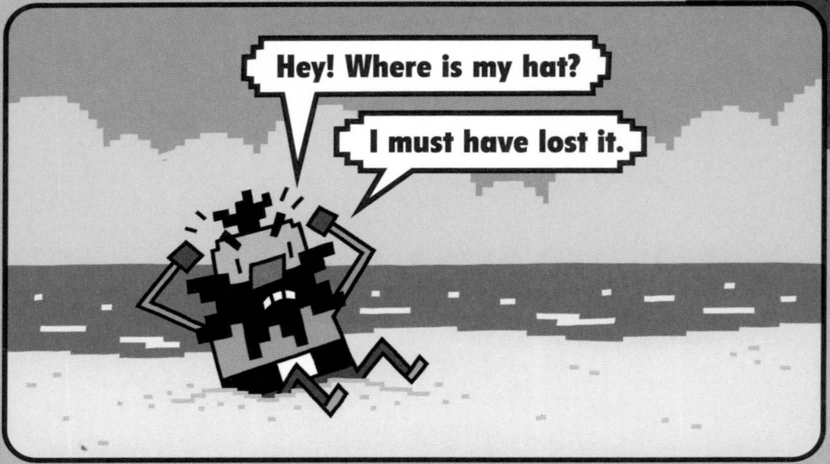
Hey! Where is my hat?
I must have lost it.

Then King Viking hears a strange roar! It is coming from the forest.

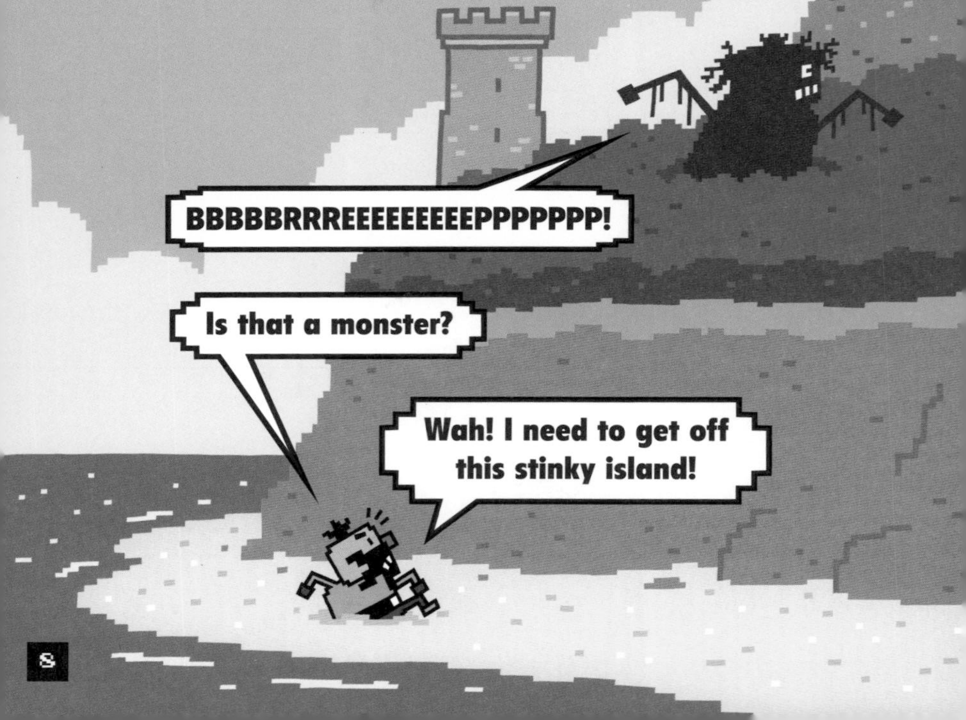
BBBBBRRREEEEEEEEEEPPPPPPP!
Is that a monster?
Wah! I need to get off this stinky island!

2 FEELING CRABBY

King Viking stands on the beach.

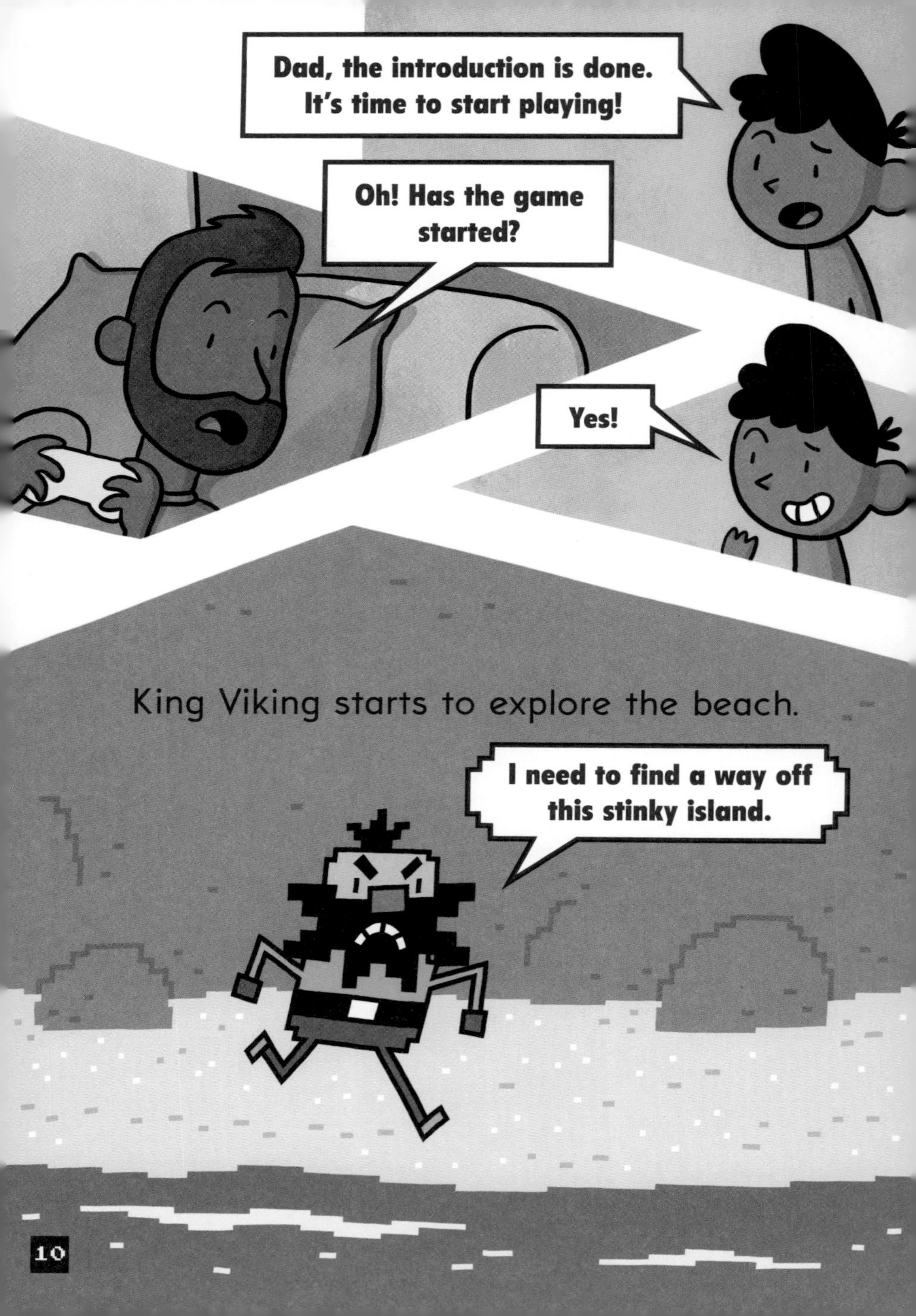
Dad, the introduction is done. It's time to start playing!
Oh! Has the game started?
Yes!
King Viking starts to explore the beach.
I need to find a way off this stinky island.

He spots some coins on the ground.

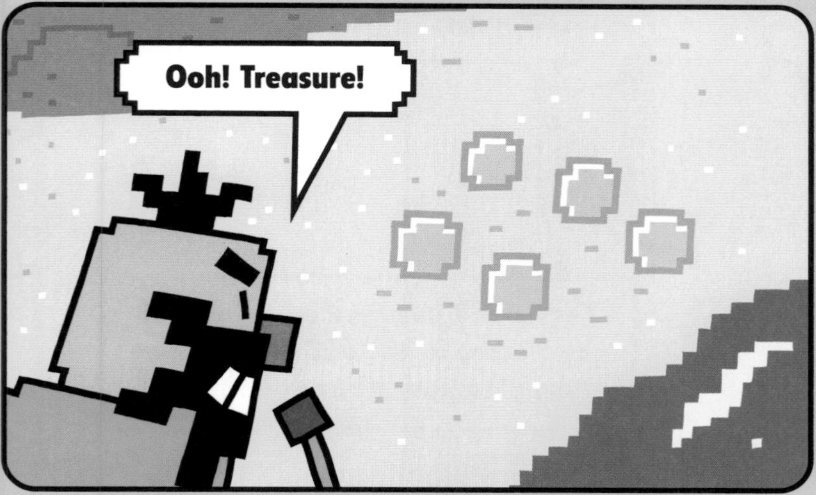
Ooh! Treasure!

He collects the coins.

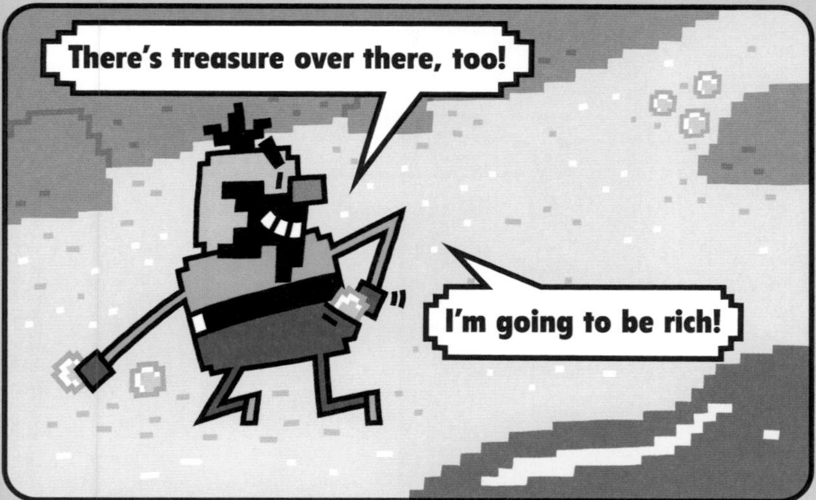
There's treasure over there, too!
I'm going to be rich!

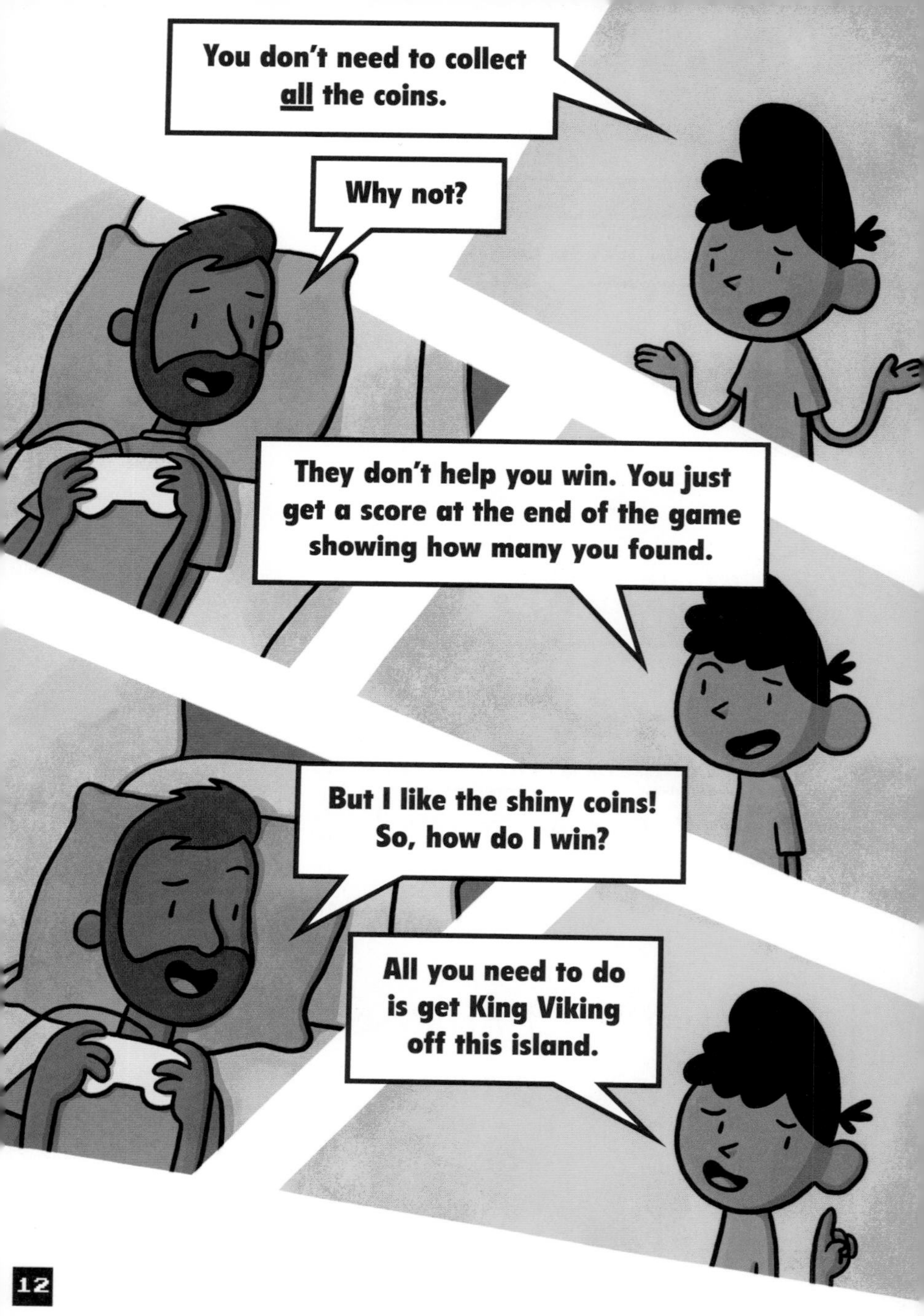
You don't need to collect all the coins.
Why not?
They don't help you win. You just get a score at the end of the game showing how many you found.
But I like the shiny coins! So, how do I win?
All you need to do is get King Viking off this island.

The beach is full of nasty crabs. King Viking avoids them.

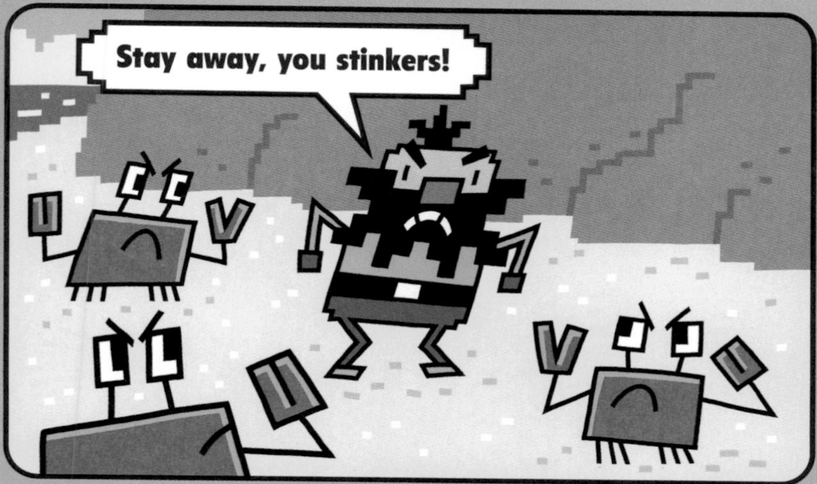
Stay away, you stinkers!

King Viking stops to grab coins. A crab sneaks up behind him.

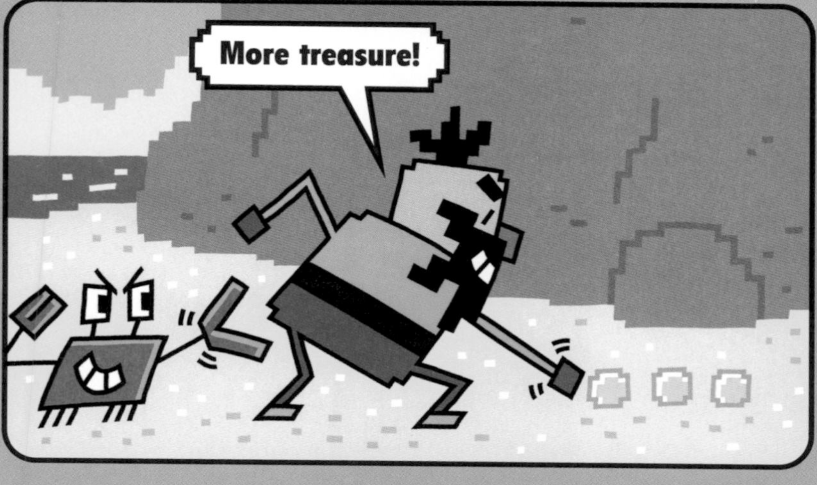
More treasure!

The crab attacks! King Viking leaps in the air. Coins fly out of his pockets.

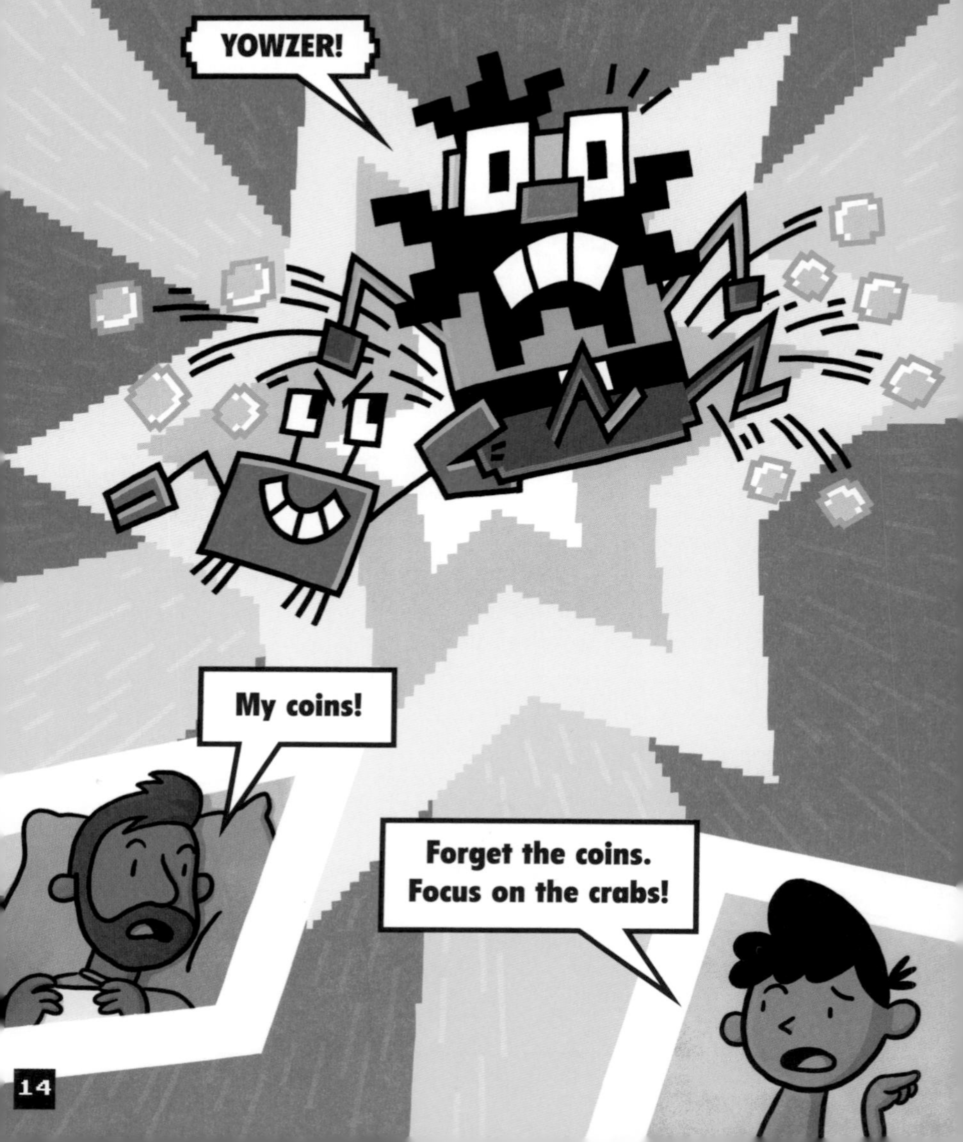
YOWZER!
My coins!
Forget the coins.
Focus on the crabs!

More crabs arrive. They snap their claws at him.

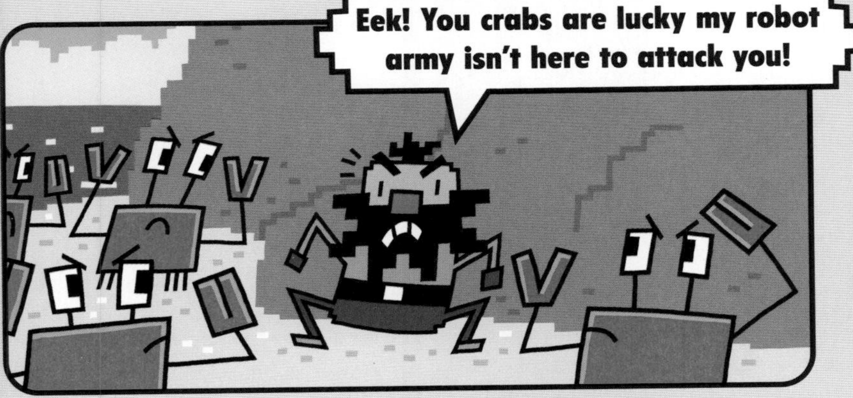
Eek! You crabs are lucky my robot army isn't here to attack you!

The crabs charge at King Viking. He climbs up a cliff to escape.

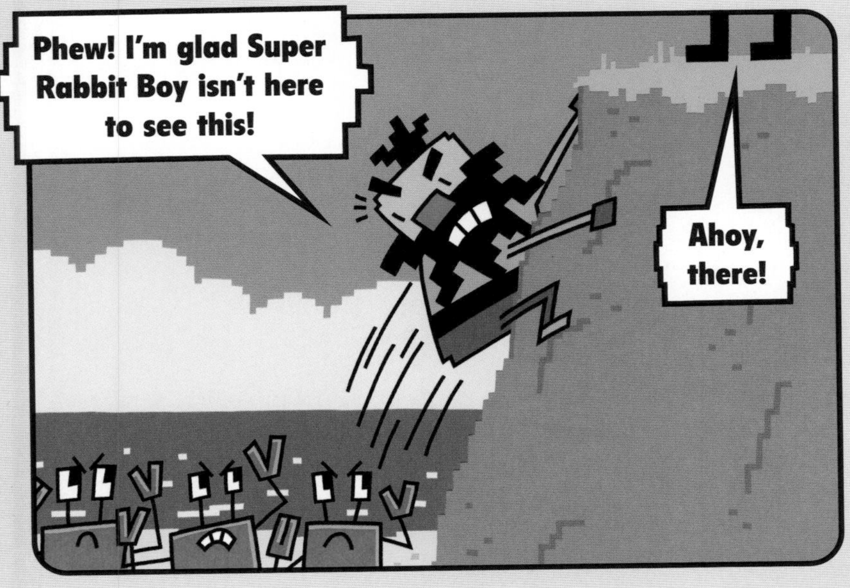
Phew! I'm glad Super Rabbit Boy isn't here to see this!
Ahoy, there!

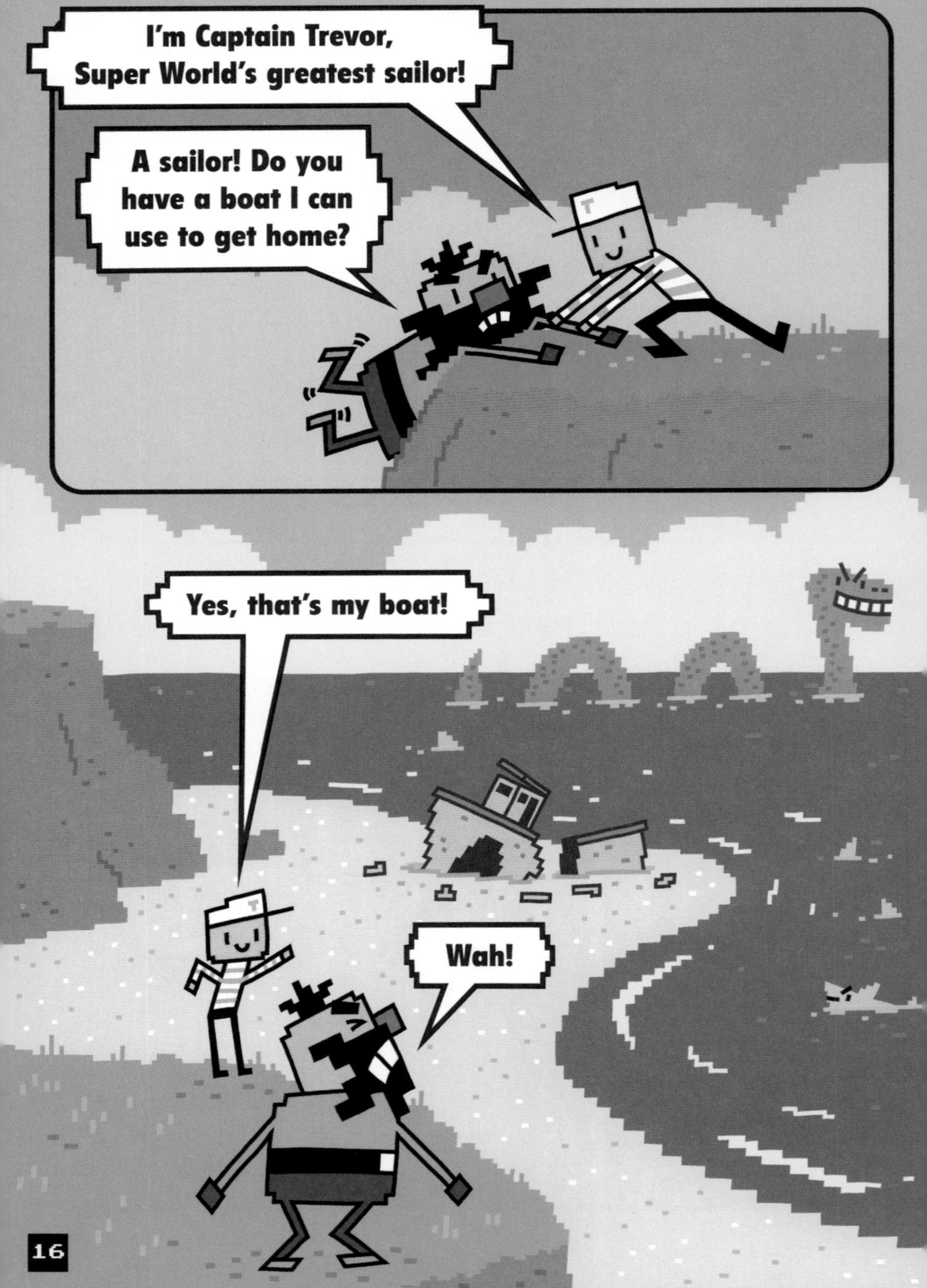
I'm Captain Trevor, Super World's greatest sailor!
A sailor! Do you have a boat I can use to get home?
Yes, that's my boat!
Wah!

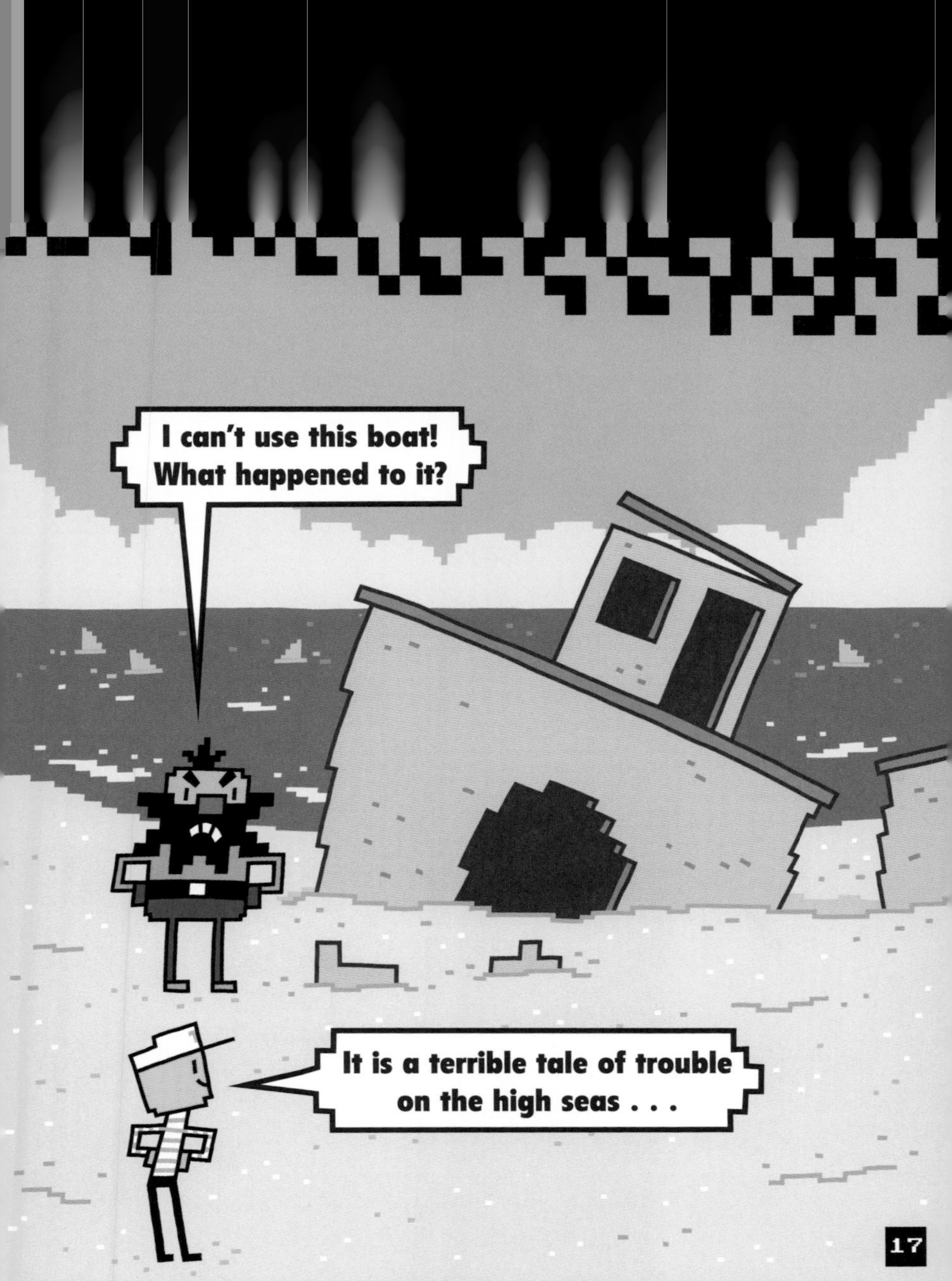
I can't use this boat! What happened to it?
It is a terrible tale of trouble on the high seas . . .

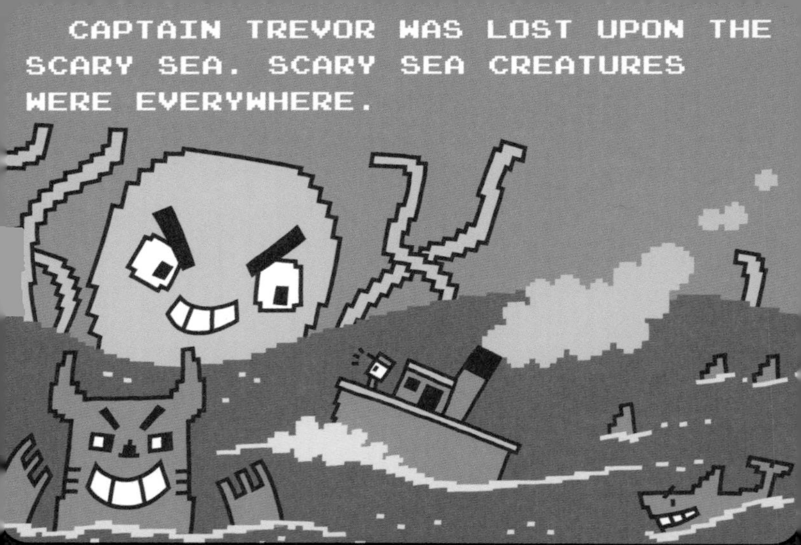
CAPTAIN TREVOR WAS LOST UPON THE SCARY SEA. SCARY SEA CREATURES WERE EVERYWHERE.

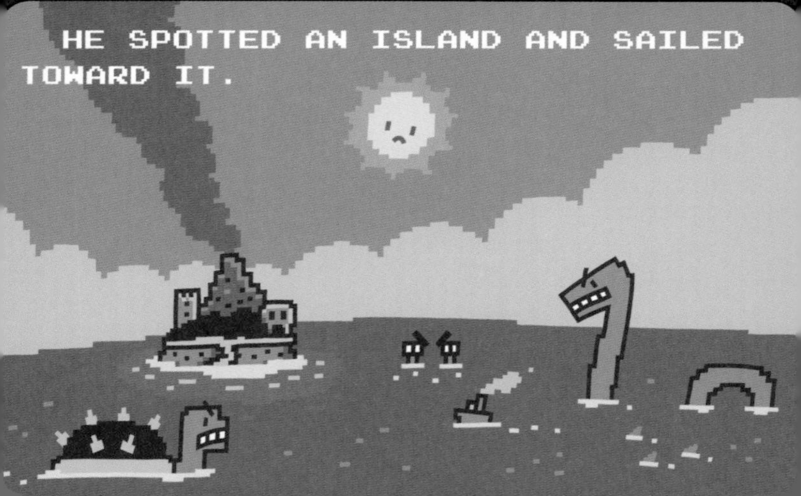
HE SPOTTED AN ISLAND AND SAILED TOWARD IT.

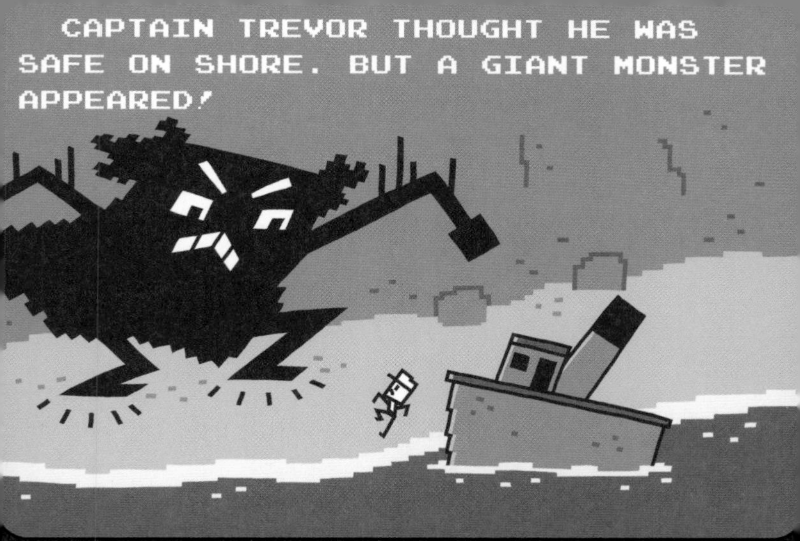
CAPTAIN TREVOR THOUGHT HE WAS SAFE ON SHORE. BUT A GIANT MONSTER APPEARED!

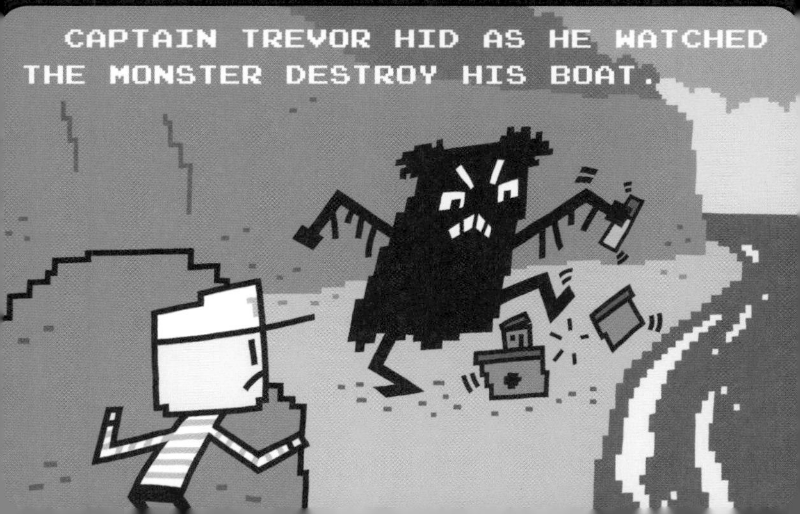
CAPTAIN TREVOR HID AS HE WATCHED THE MONSTER DESTROY HIS BOAT.

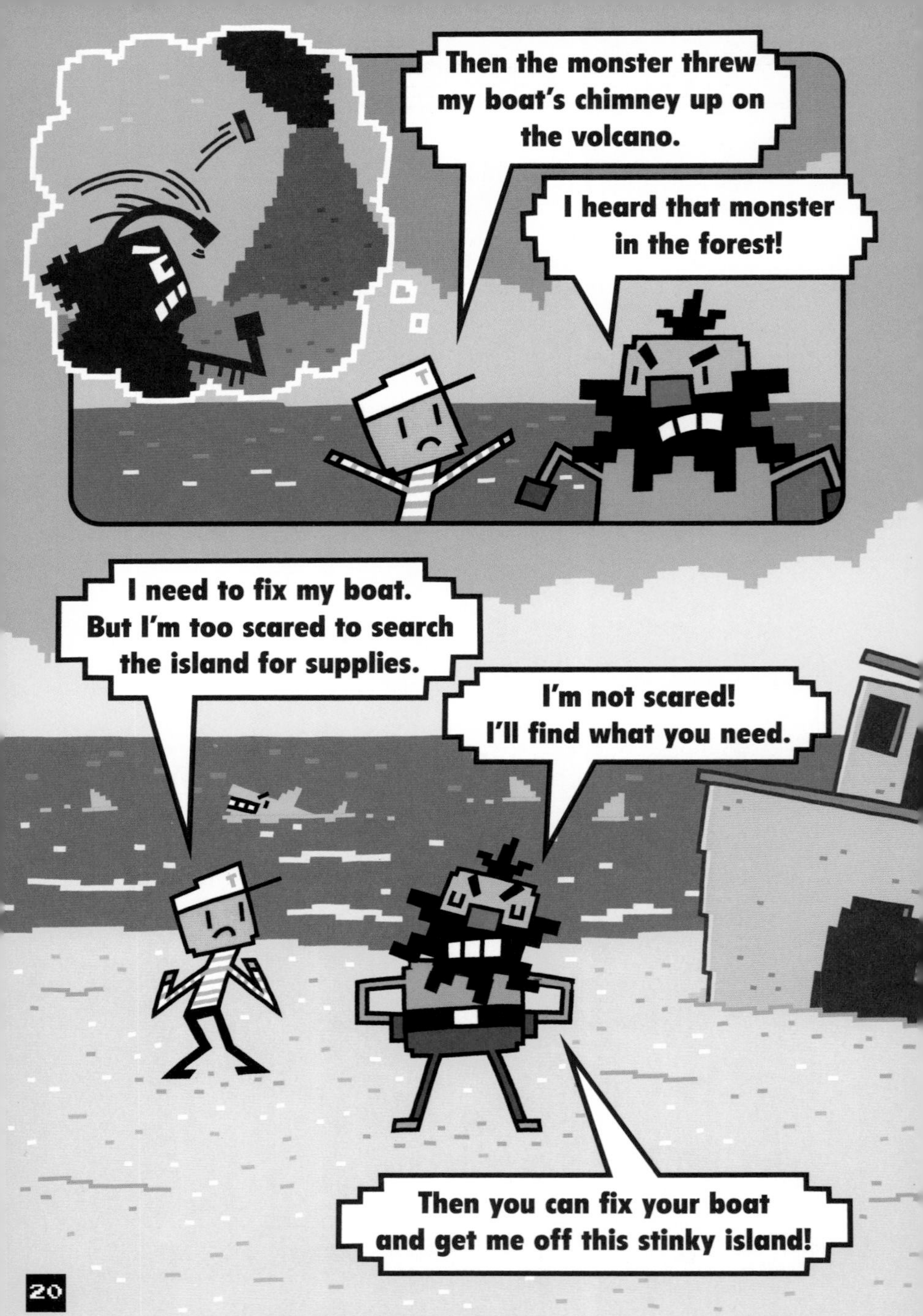
Then the monster threw my boat's chimney up on the volcano.
I heard that monster in the forest!
I need to fix my boat. But I'm too scared to search the island for supplies.
I'm not scared! I'll find what you need.
Then you can fix your boat and get me off this stinky island!

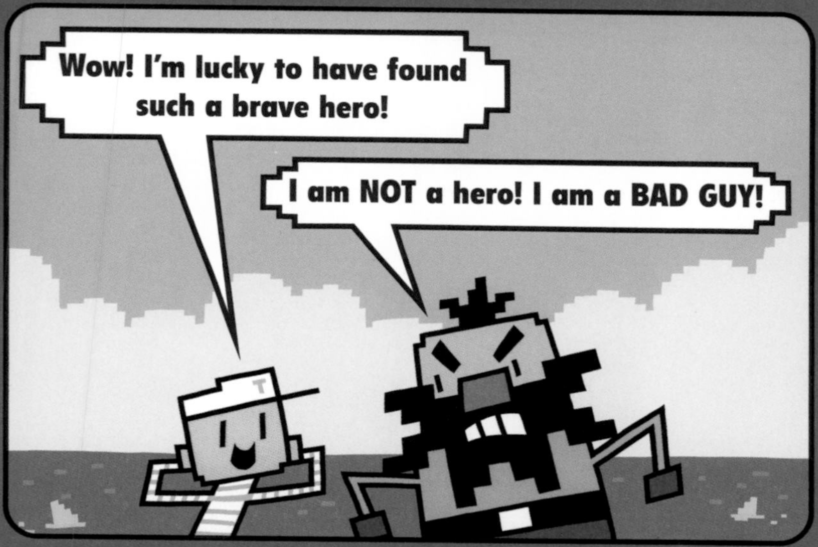
Wow! I'm lucky to have found such a brave hero!
I am NOT a hero! I am a BAD GUY!

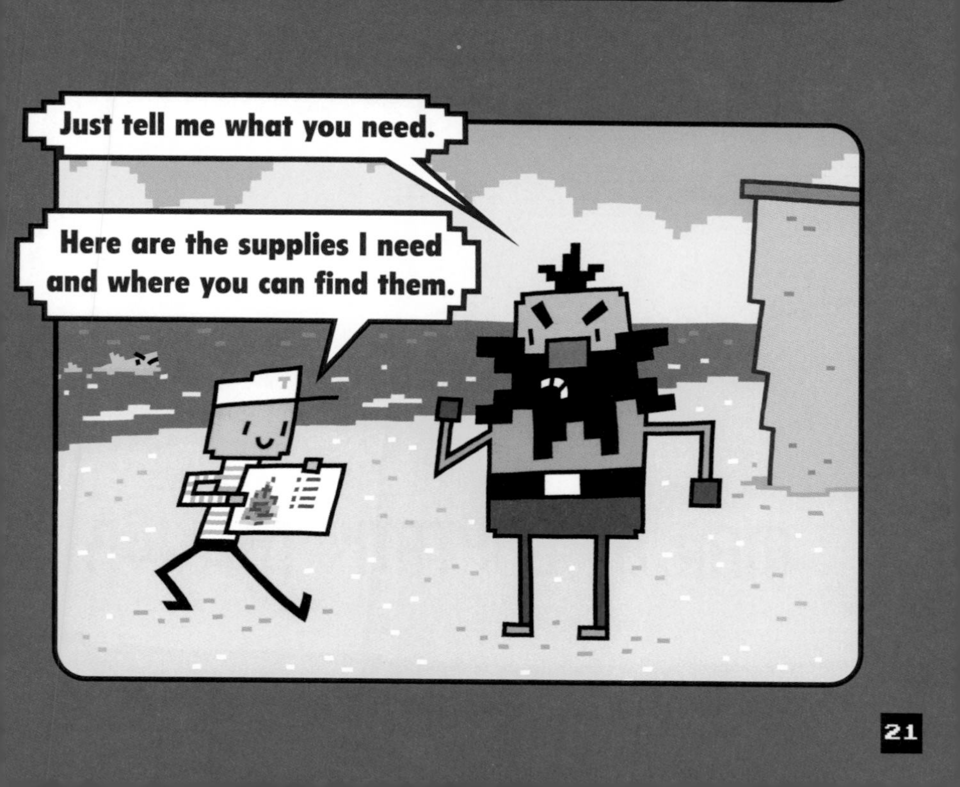
Just tell me what you need.
Here are the supplies I need and where you can find them.

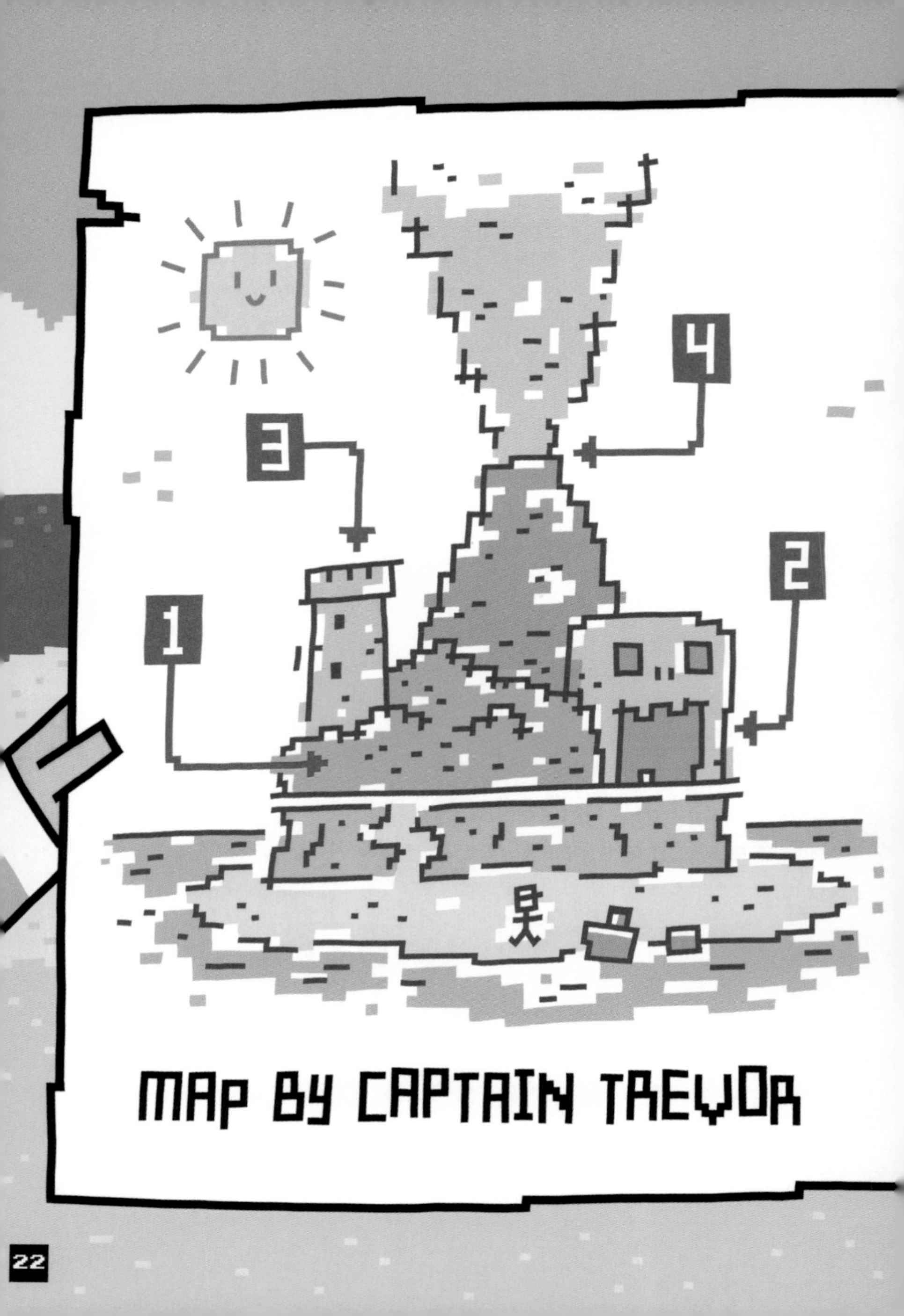
1
2
3
4

MAP BY CAPTAIN TREVOR

1  Collect wood in the forest to patch the boat.

2 Grab coal from the cave to use as fuel.

3  Find the sea map hidden in the Old Fortress to learn a safe way across the Scary Sea.

4 Get the chimney from the volcano so the boat's steam engine will work.

King Viking sets off in search of everything they need.

Wow! What a lovely and kind man!

4 MONKEY BUSINESS

King Viking starts his search in the forest.

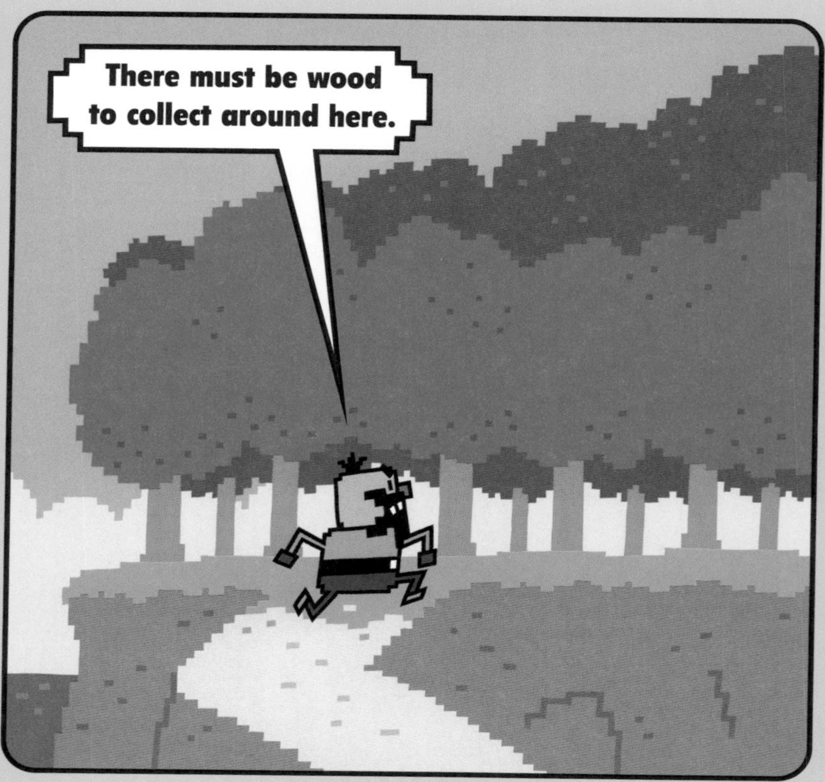
There must be wood to collect around here.

He doesn't see any wood on the ground. But he does find coins.

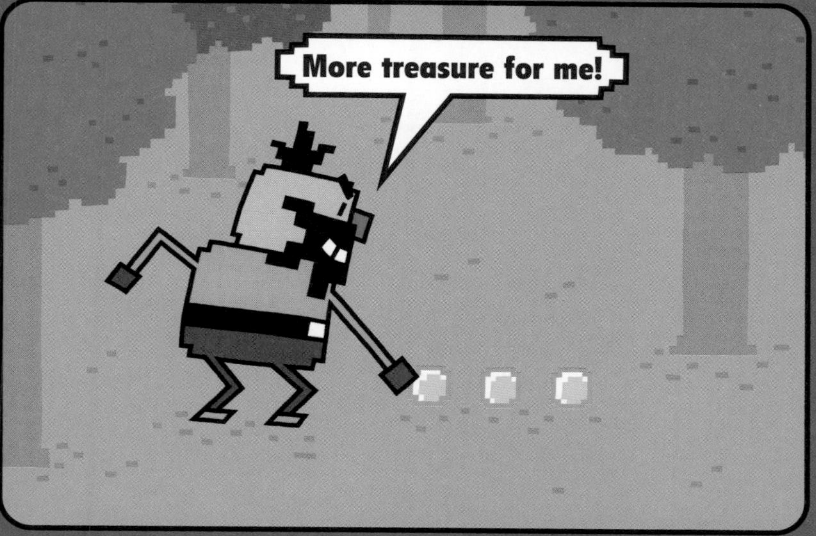
More treasure for me!

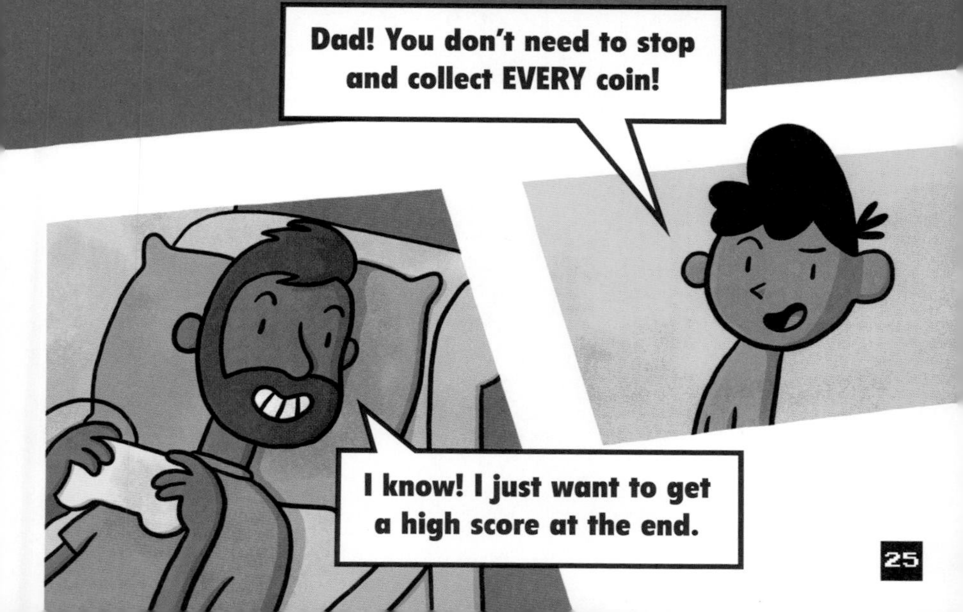
Dad! You don't need to stop and collect EVERY coin!
I know! I just want to get a high score at the end.

King Viking finds a fallen log under a tree. He collects the wood.

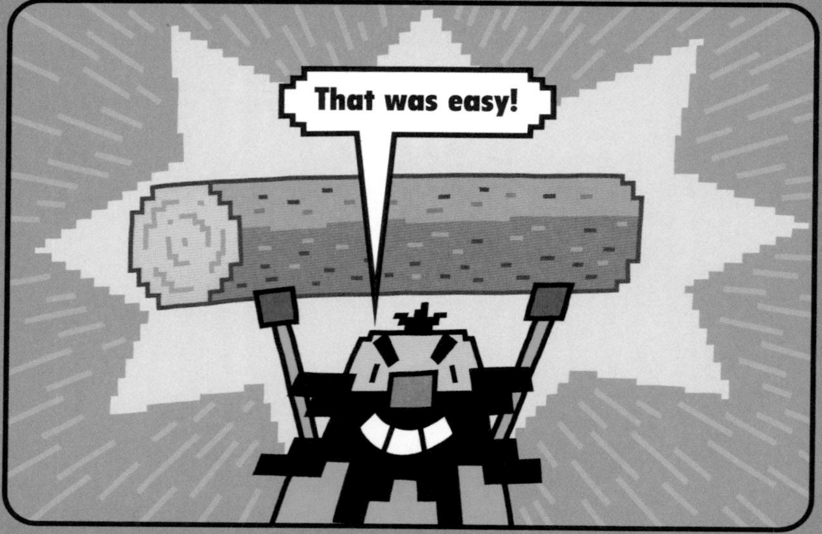
That was easy!

Suddenly, a stone hits him on the head.

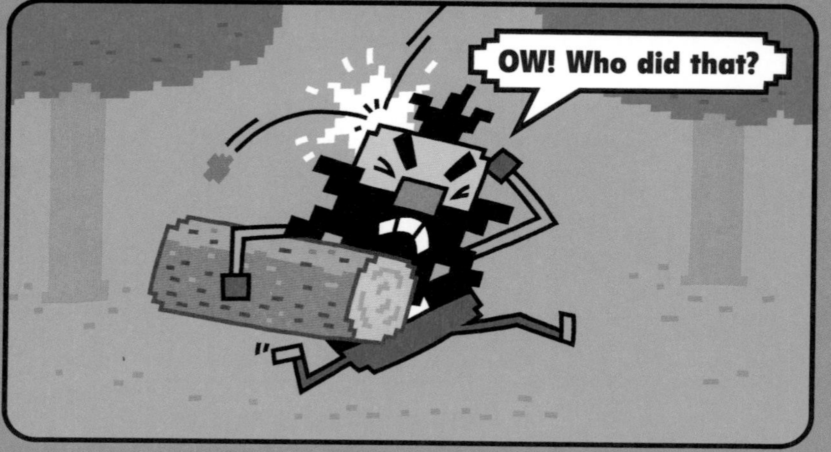
OW! Who did that?

King Viking spots a monkey in a tree. The monkey is angry that King Viking is stealing the log.

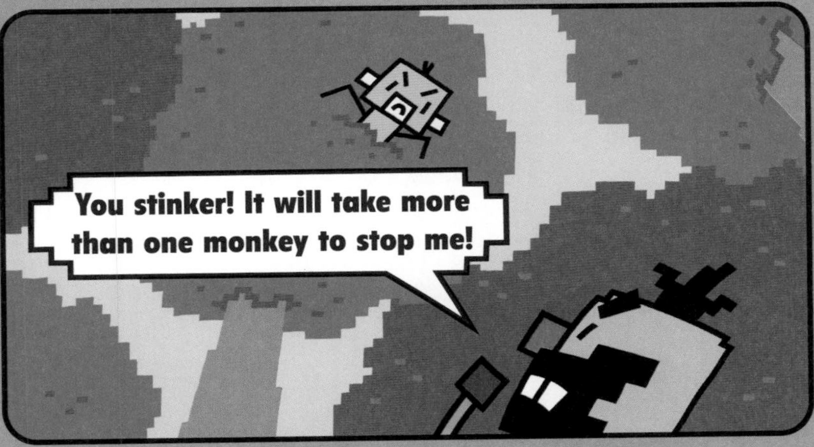
You stinker! It will take more than one monkey to stop me!

King Viking looks all around. He is surrounded by monkeys!

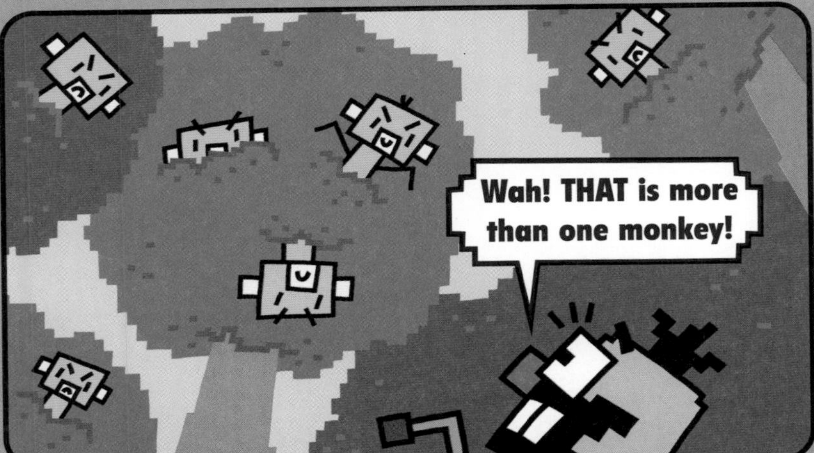
Wah! THAT is more than one monkey!

The monkeys throw sticks and stones at King Viking. He dodges them and runs away.

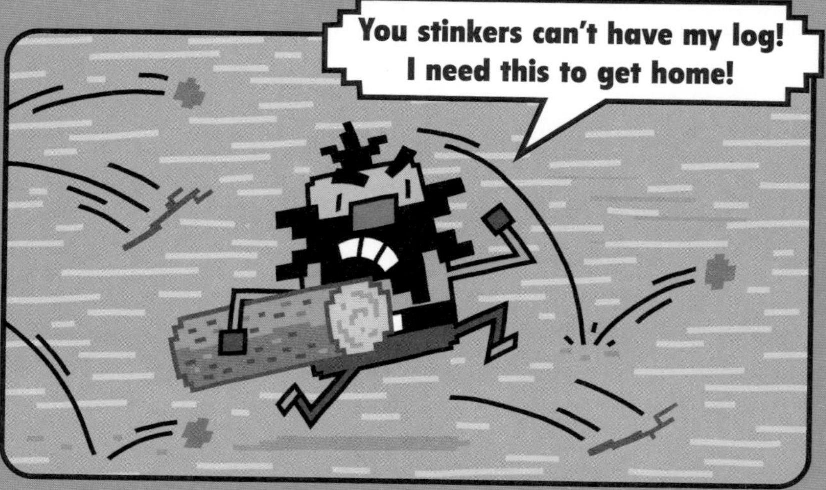
You stinkers can't have my log! I need this to get home!

But then King Viking sees coins. He stops to gather them.

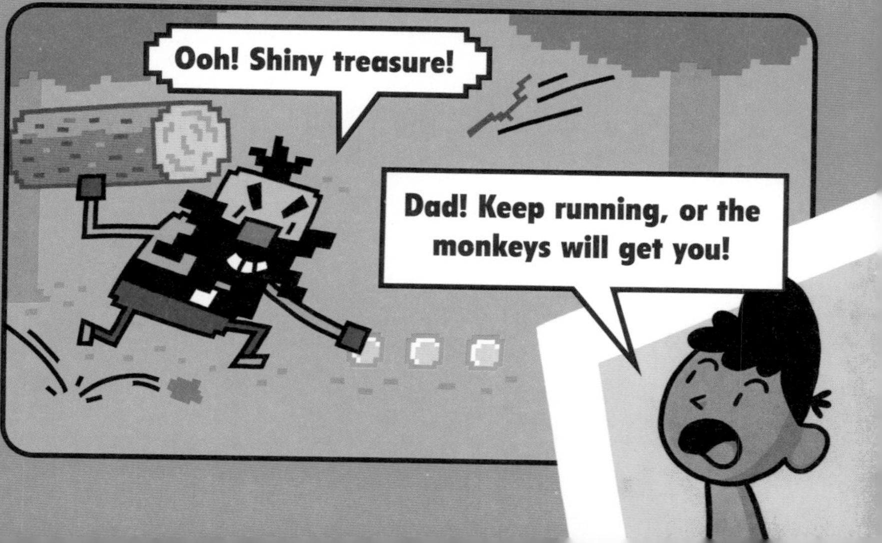
Ooh! Shiny treasure!
Dad! Keep running, or the monkeys will get you!

King Viking is almost back at the beach when a big stone slams into his back.

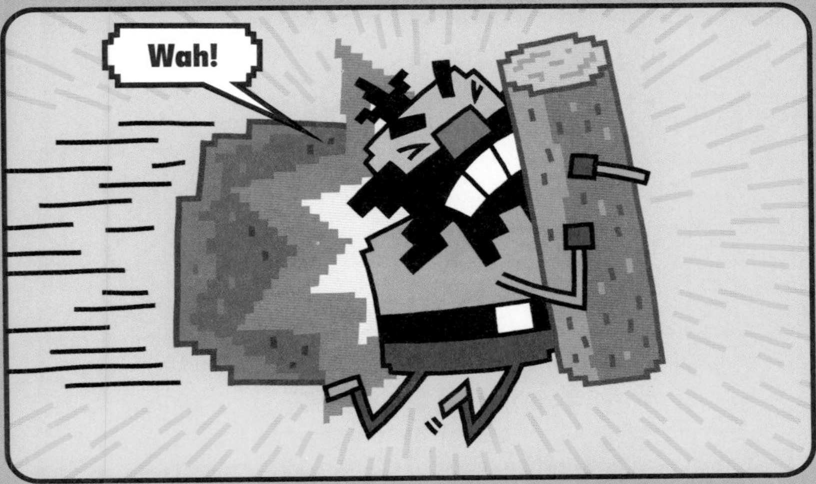
Wah!

He is sent flying through the trees!

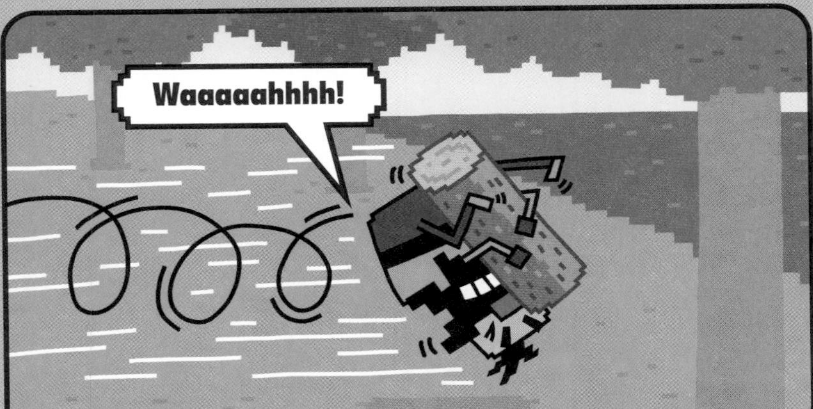
Waaaaahhhh!

Captain Trevor is surprised to see King Viking fly out of the forest.

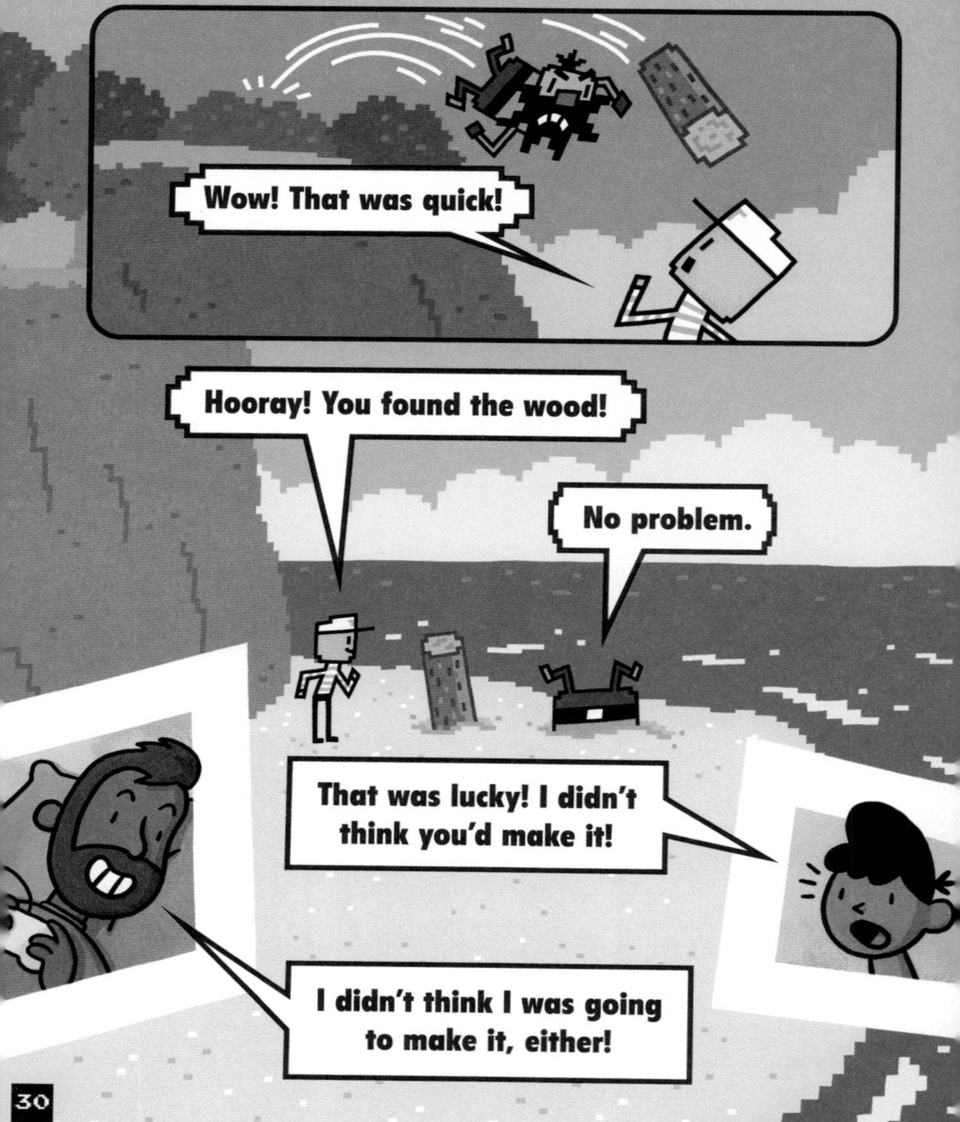
Wow! That was quick!
Hooray! You found the wood!
No problem.
That was lucky! I didn't think you'd make it!
I didn't think I was going to make it, either!

DANGER IN THE DARK

King Viking goes to the cave next.

Now I need to grab the coal.

It is very dark in the cave.

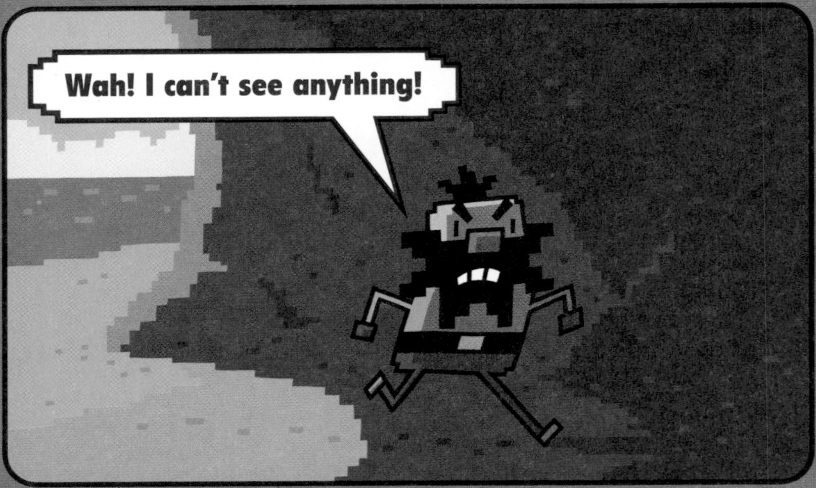
Wah! I can't see anything!

King Viking stumbles through the darkness.

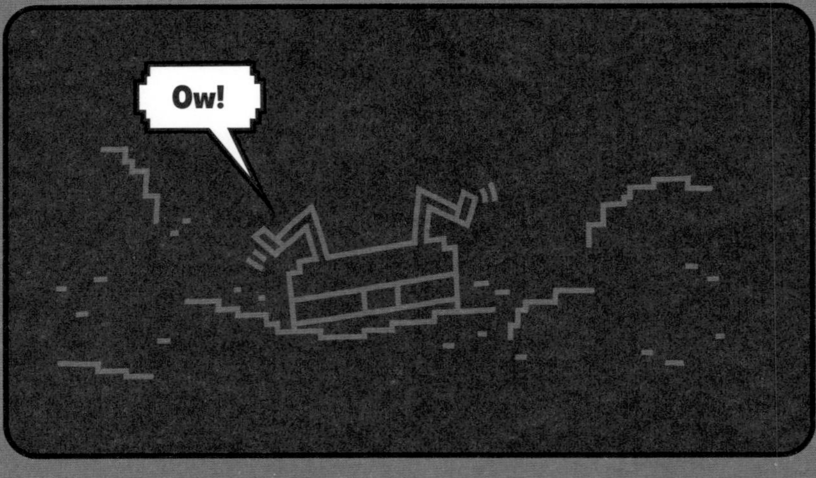
Ow!

At last he spots something familiar.

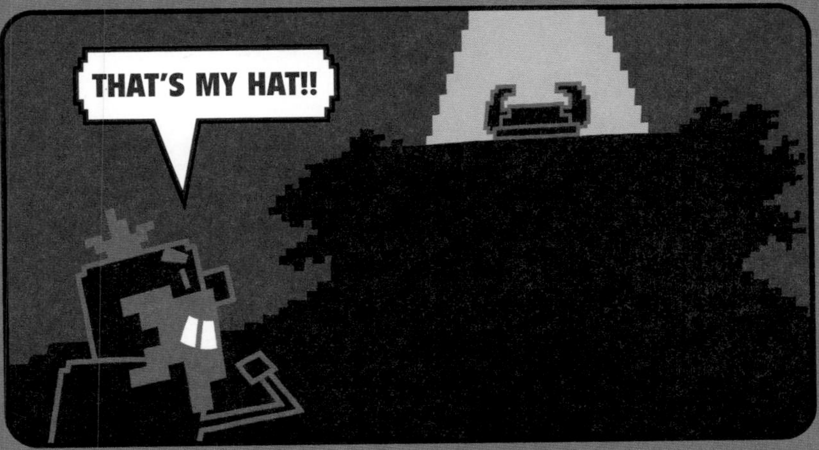
THAT'S MY HAT!!

Suddenly, the room starts to rumble and shake. King Viking has woken up the island's monster. It is wearing his hat!

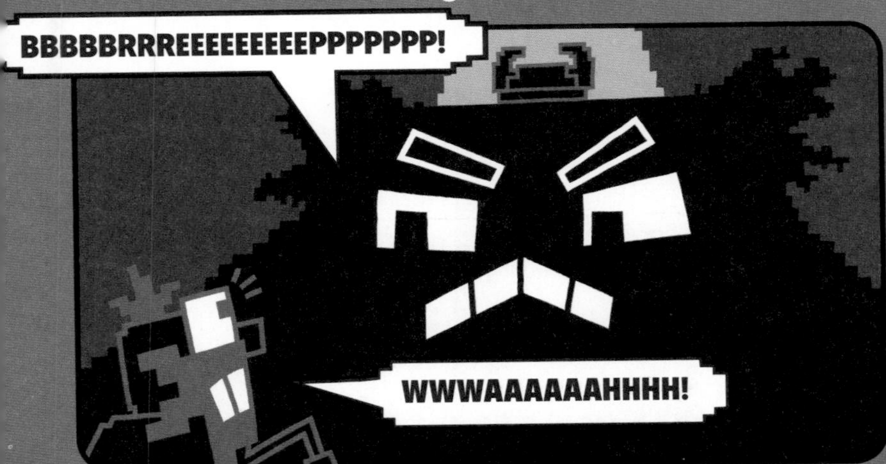
BBBBBRRREEEEEEEEEEPPPPPPP!
WWWAAAAAAHHHH!

The monster's glowing eyes light up the whole cave. King Viking can now see a big lump of coal.

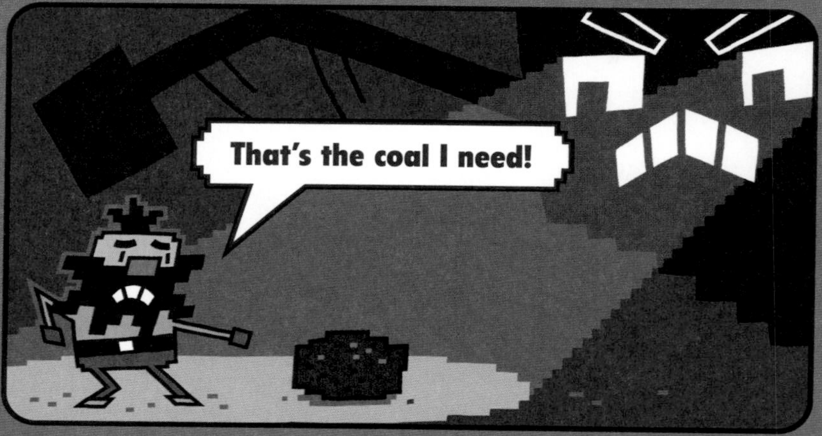
That's the coal I need!

King Viking grabs it and runs out of the cave. But the monster is right behind him!

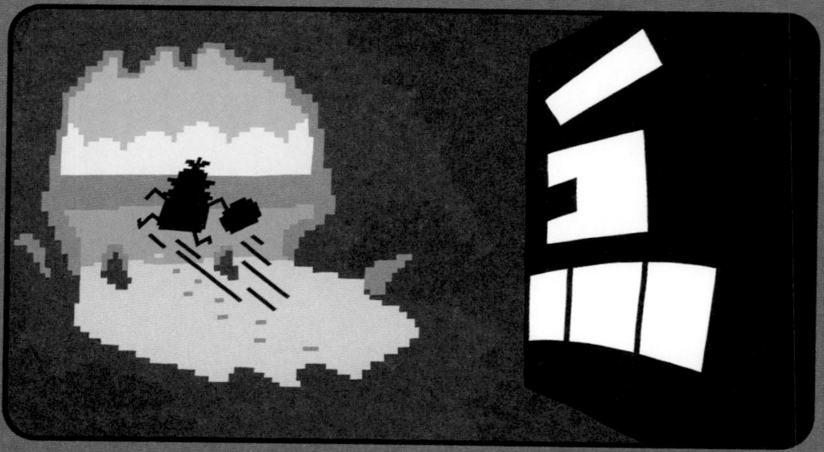

King Viking spots some coins near a large rock.

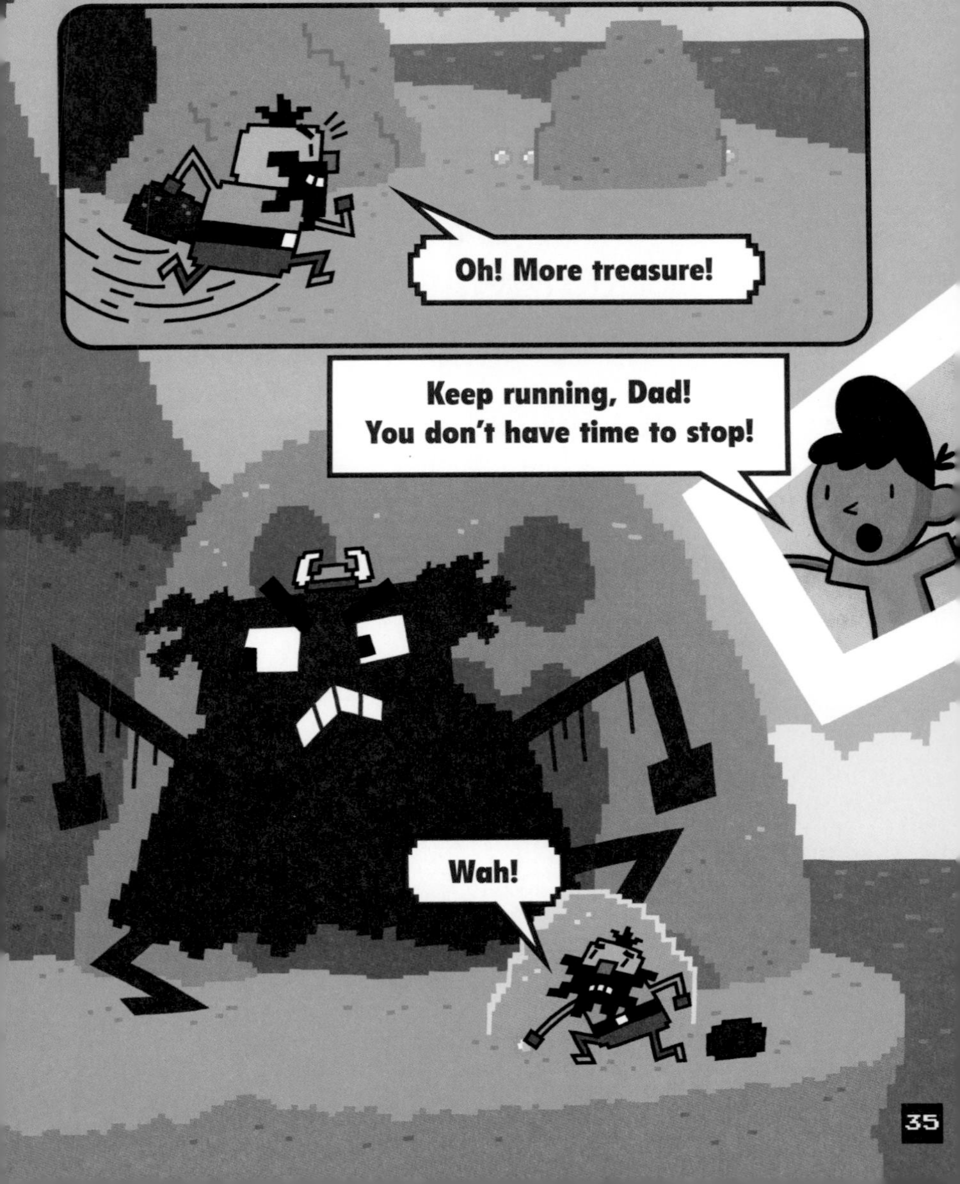
Oh! More treasure!
Keep running, Dad!
You don't have time to stop!
Wah!

King Viking hides behind the rock. He is scared the monster will find him.

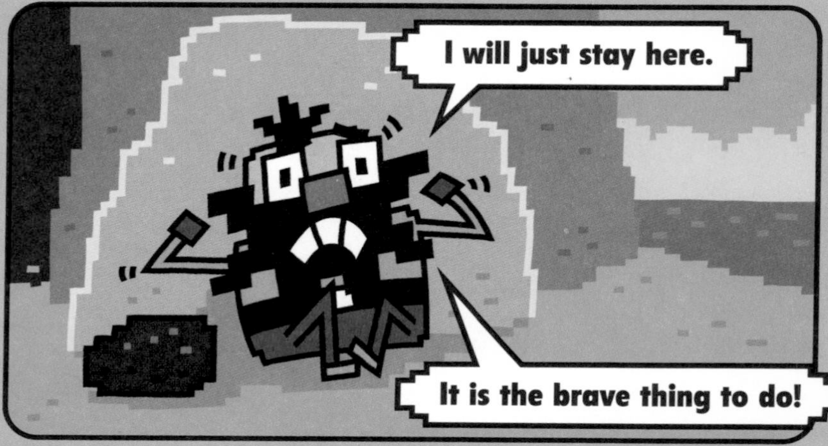
I will just stay here.
It is the brave thing to do!

When he finally looks up, the monster is gone.

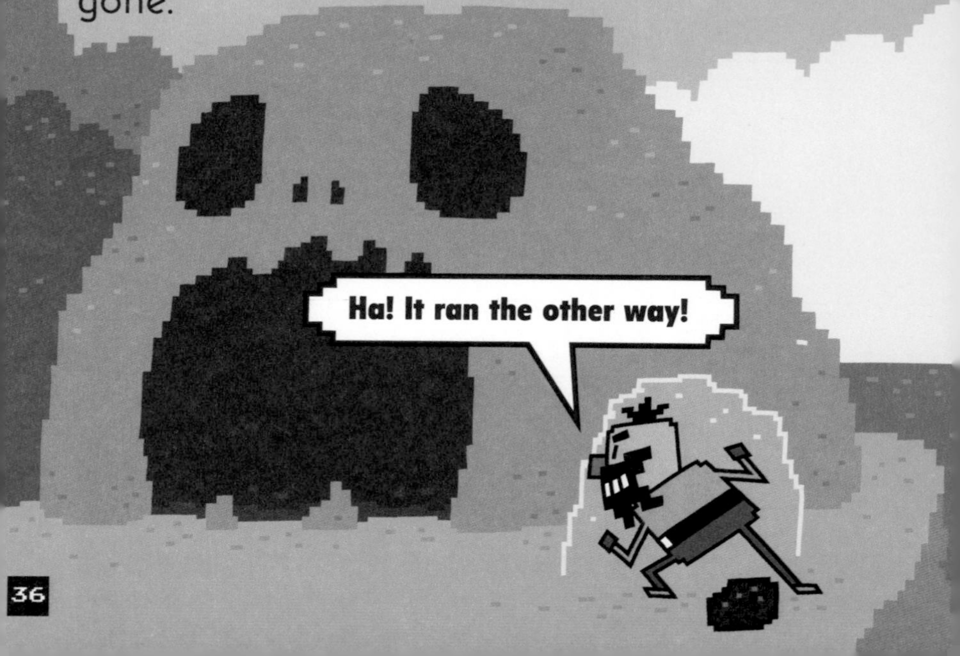
Ha! It ran the other way!

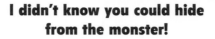

I didn't know you could hide from the monster!

When in doubt, hide out!

Back on the beach, King Viking gives the coal to Captain Trevor. He spots the monster climbing up the volcano.

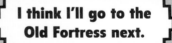

I think I'll go to the Old Fortress next.

6 THE FORTRESS OF FEAR

King Viking arrives at the Old Fortress.

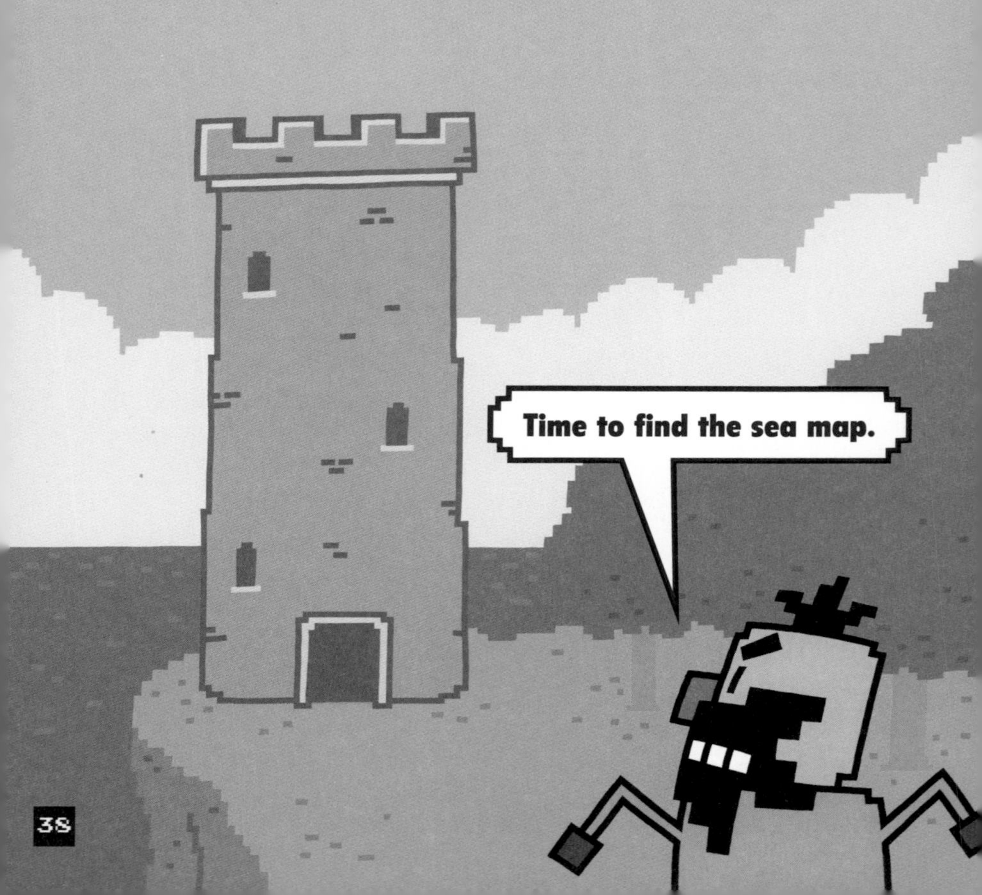
Time to find the sea map.

It is cold, damp, and smelly inside the Old Fortress.

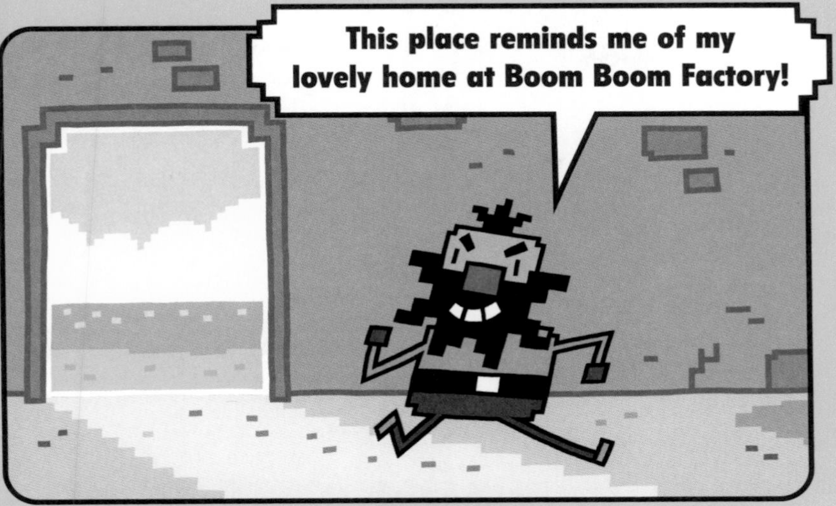
This place reminds me of my lovely home at Boom Boom Factory!

King Viking starts to explore. There is no sign of the map. But he DOES find coins!

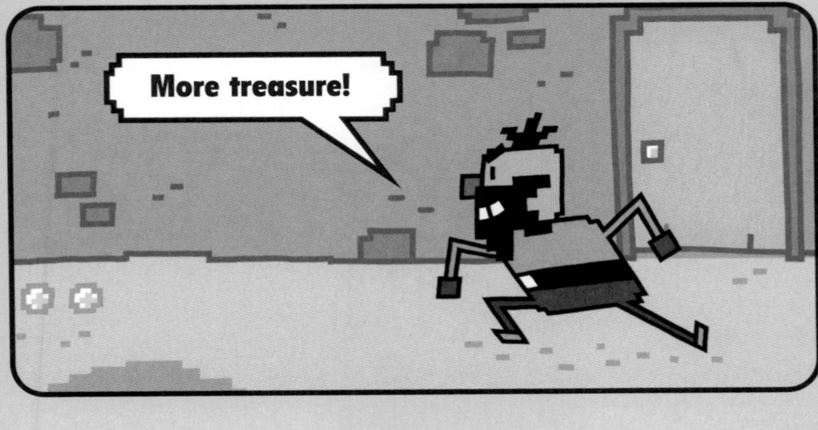
More treasure!

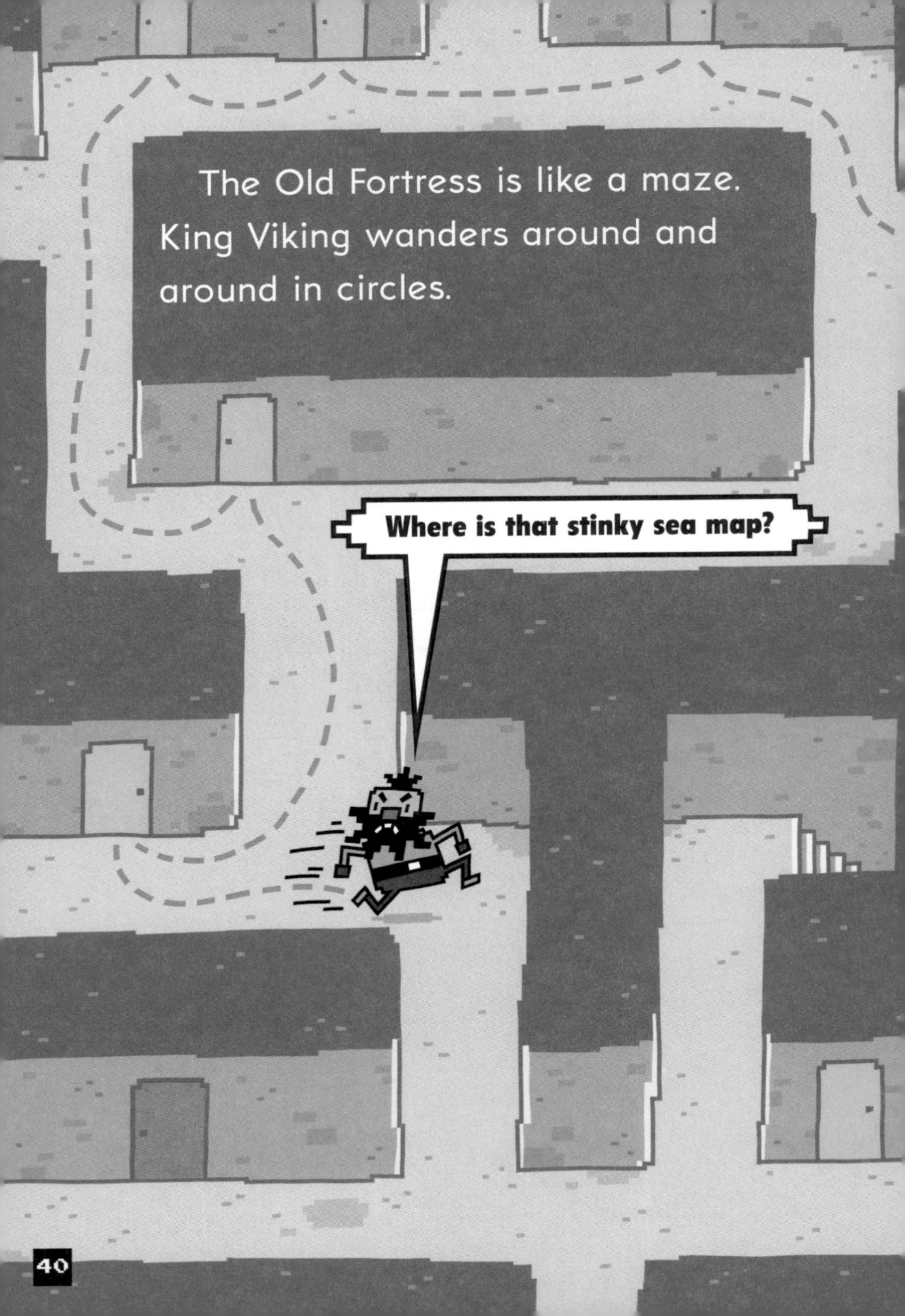
The Old Fortress is like a maze. King Viking wanders around and around in circles.
Where is that stinky sea map?

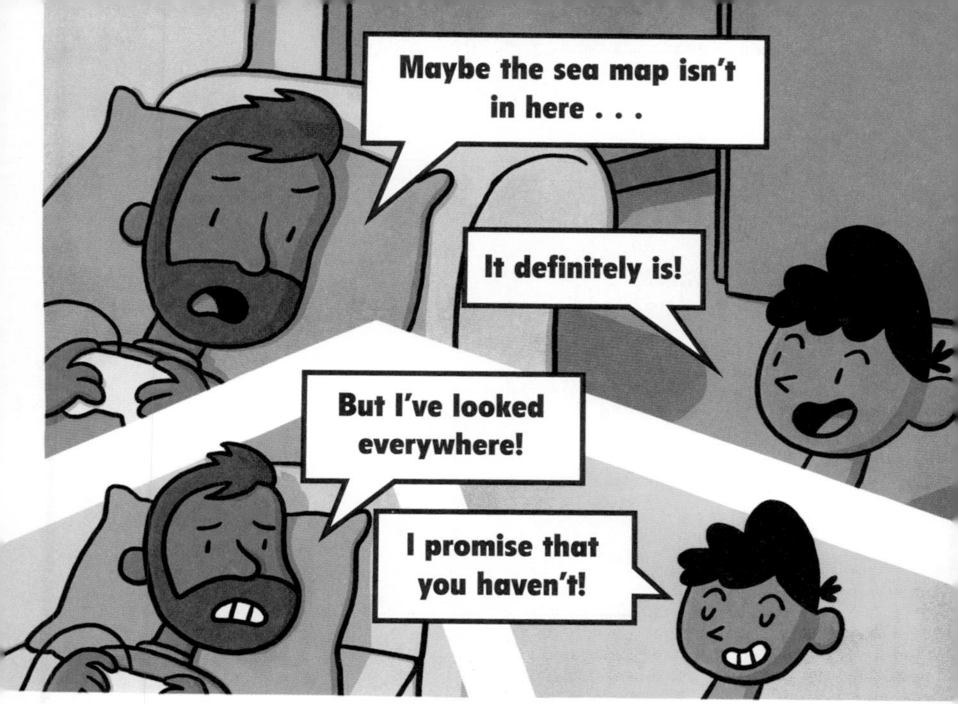
Maybe the sea map isn't in here . . .
It definitely is!
But I've looked everywhere!
I promise that you haven't!

King Viking is getting very grumpy.

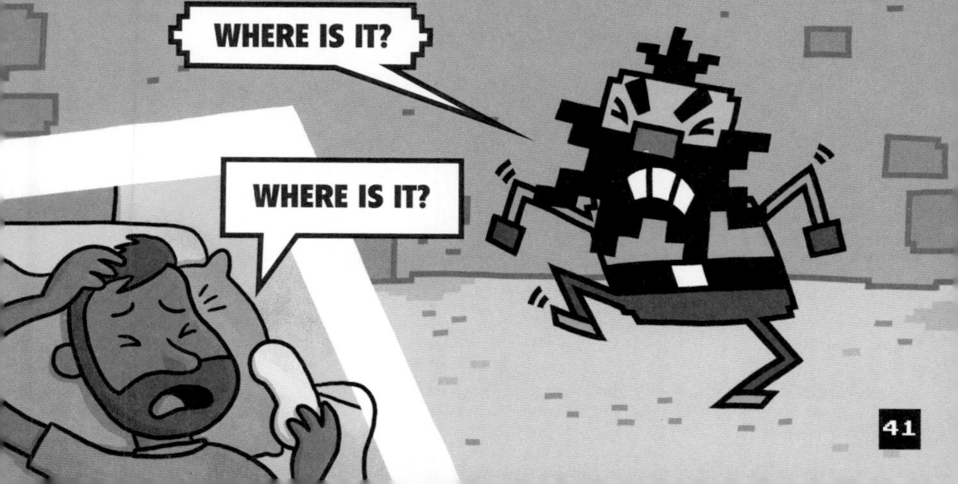
WHERE IS IT?
WHERE IS IT?

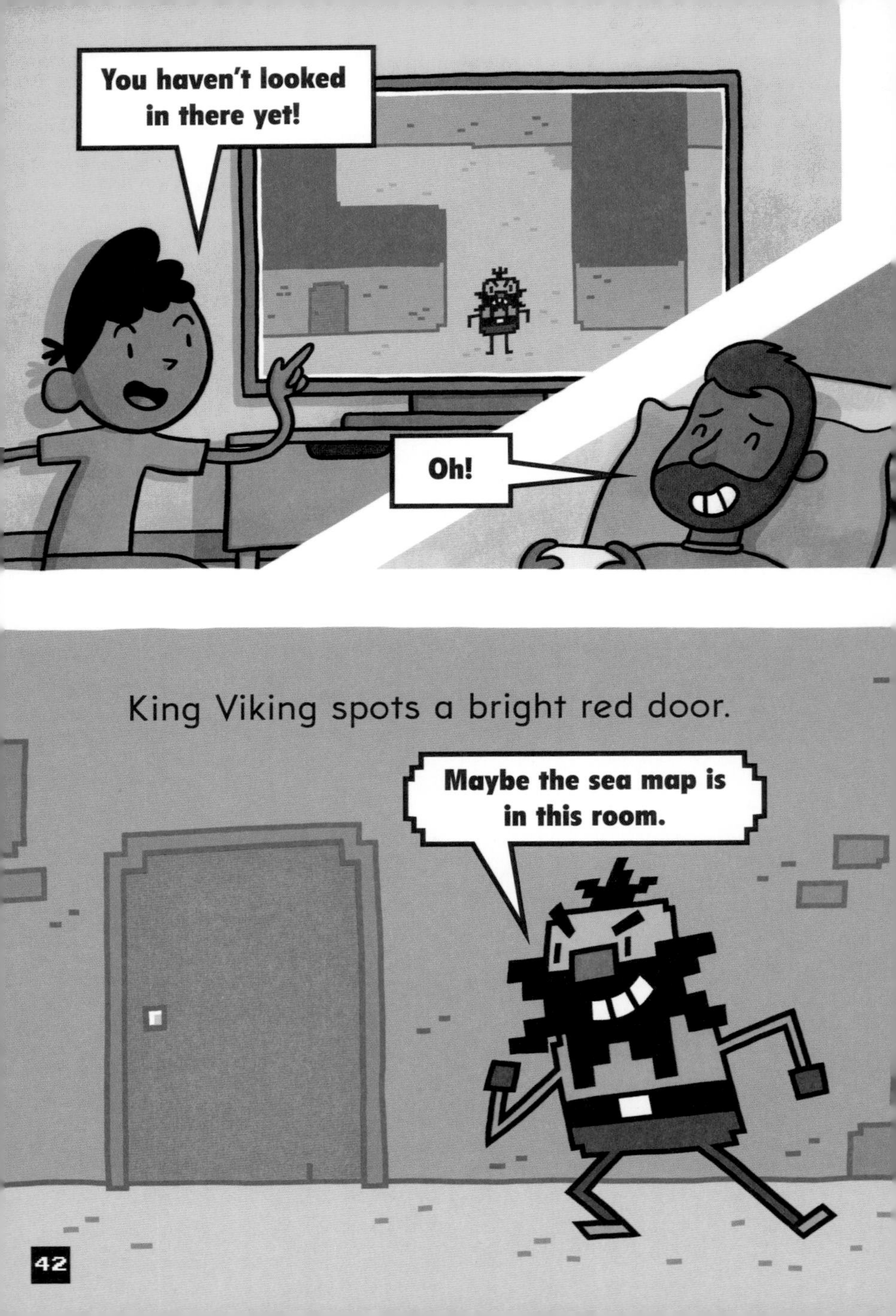
You haven't looked in there yet!
Oh!
King Viking spots a bright red door.
Maybe the sea map is in this room.

King Viking steps inside and finds the map.

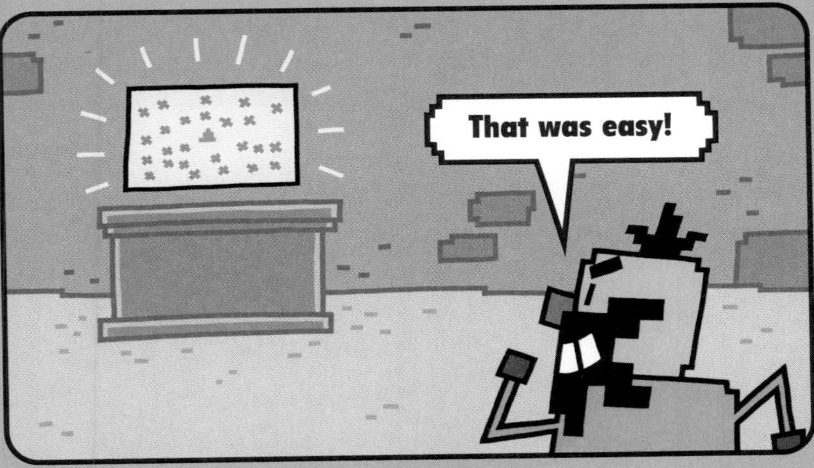
That was easy!

But as soon as King Viking grabs the sea map, he gets a surprise.

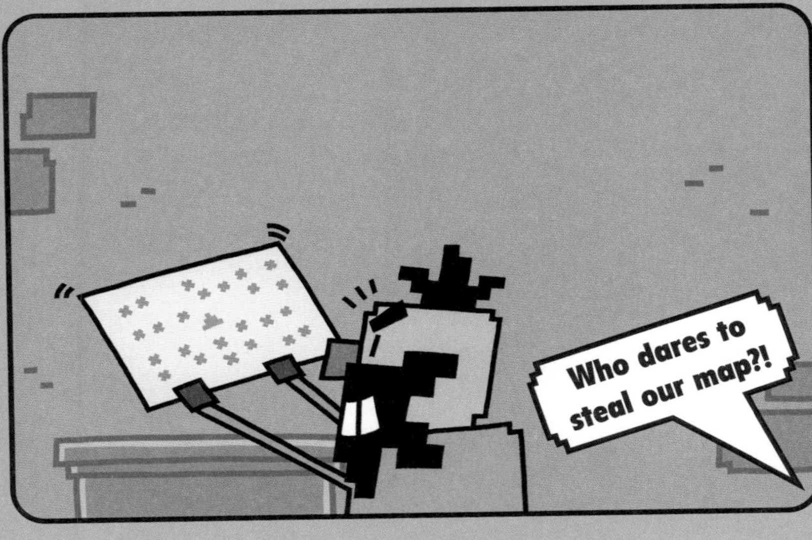
Who dares to steal our map?!

The room fills with angry Pirate Ghosts!

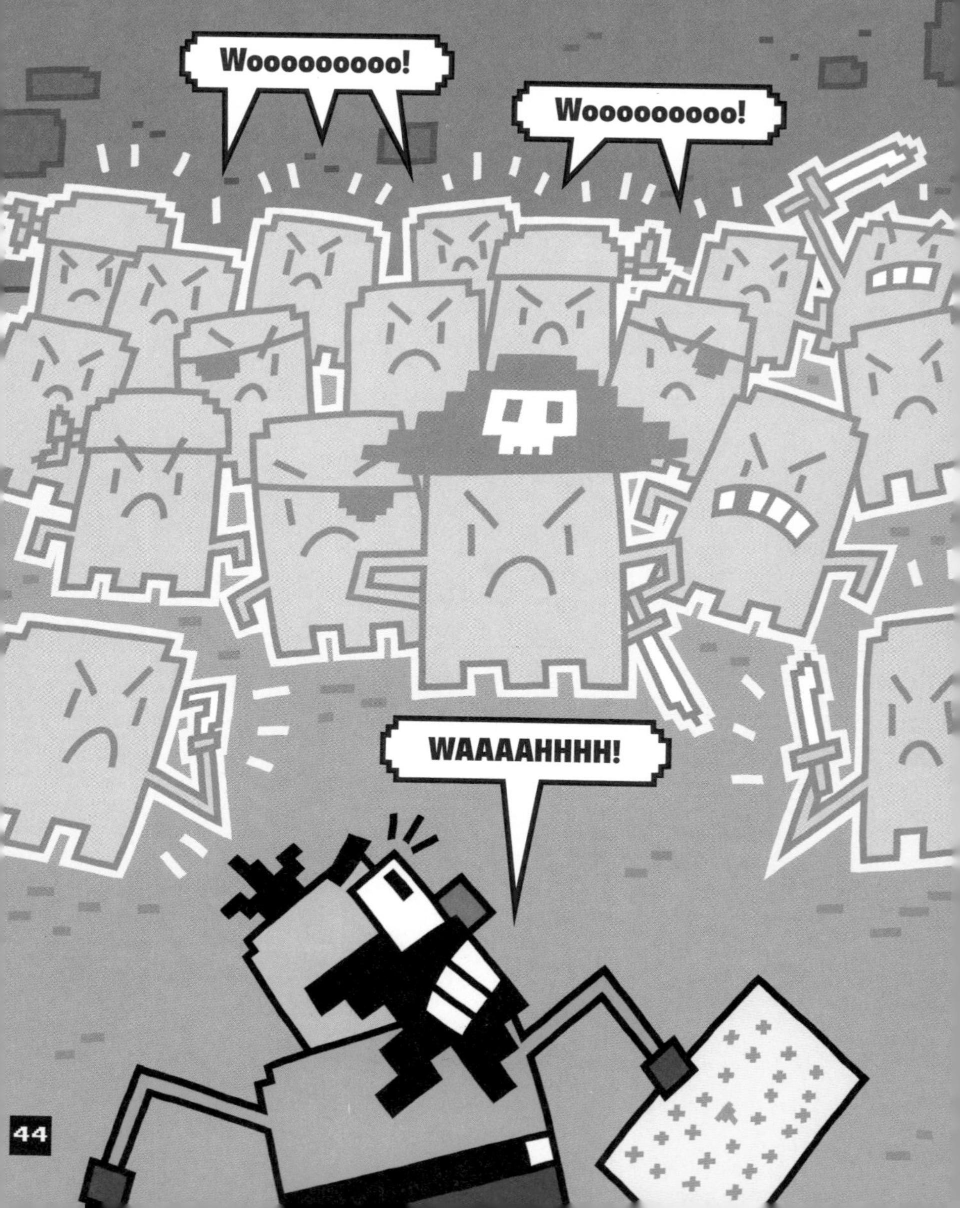
Wooooooooo!
Wooooooooo!
WAAAAHHHH!

7 A WINDOW OF OPPORTUNITY

King Viking runs out of the room. The Pirate Ghosts chase after him.

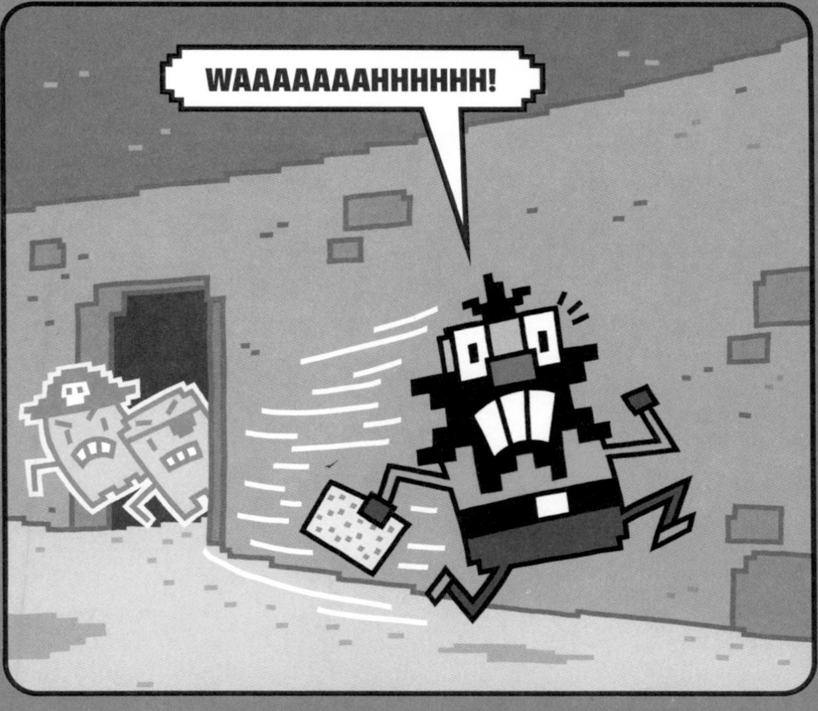
WAAAAAAAHHHHHH!

King Viking can't find his way out of the Old Fortress. Pirate Ghosts lurk around every turn.

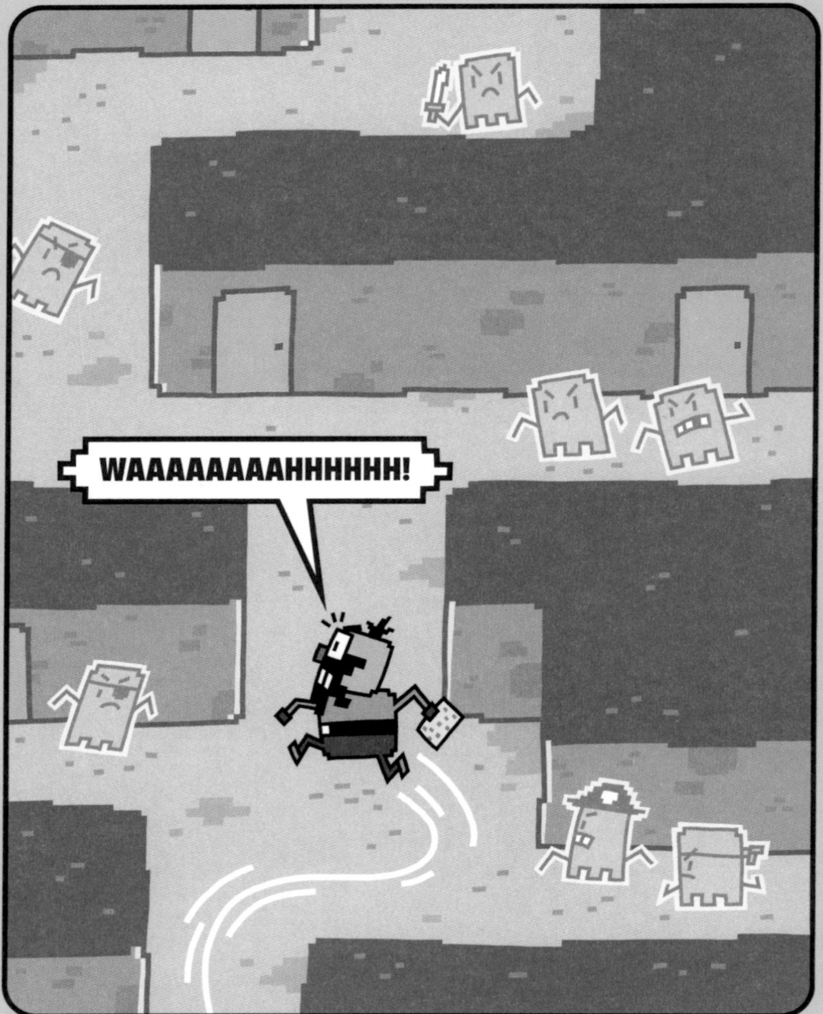
WAAAAAAAAHHHHHH!

He finally spots the exit and starts to run toward it . . .

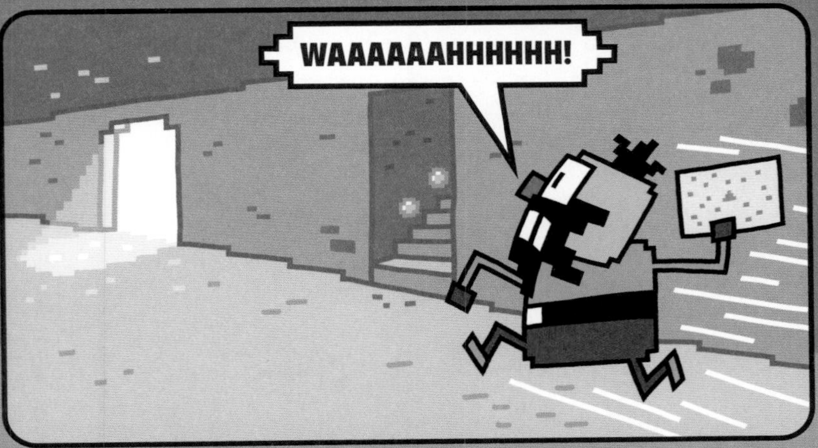
WAAAAAAHHHHHH!

But then he sees some coins.

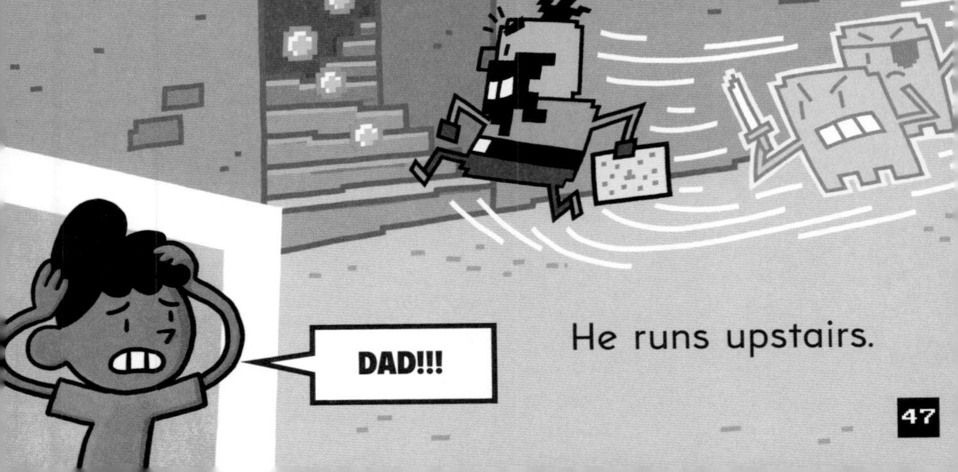
Ooh! Shiny treasure!
DAD!!!

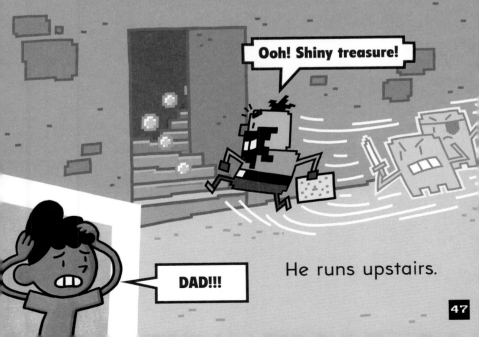

He runs upstairs.

King Viking is now completely surrounded by Pirate Ghosts.

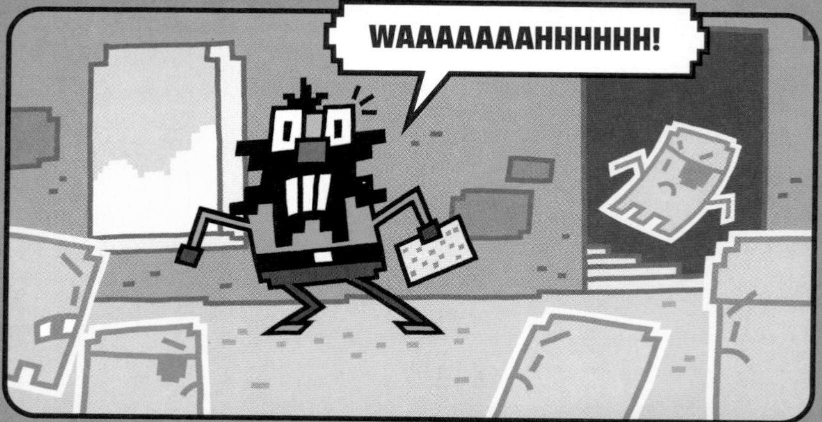
WAAAAAAAHHHHHH!

King Viking is trapped. He stumbles backward and falls out the window.

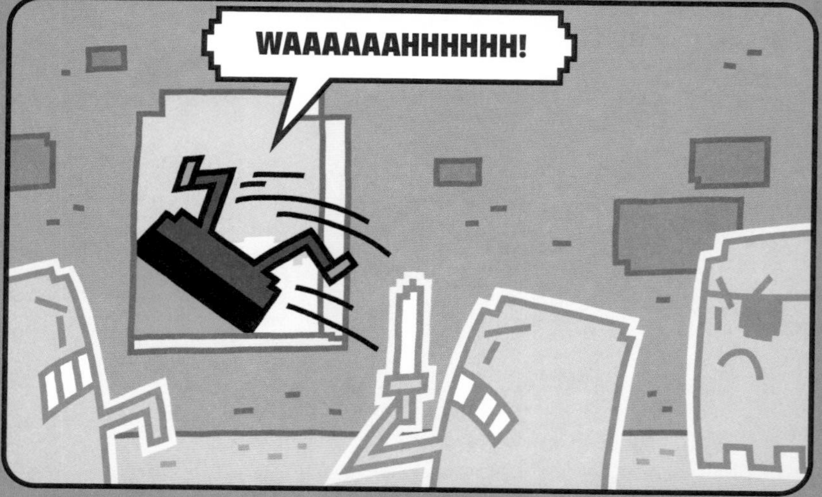
WAAAAAAHHHHHH!

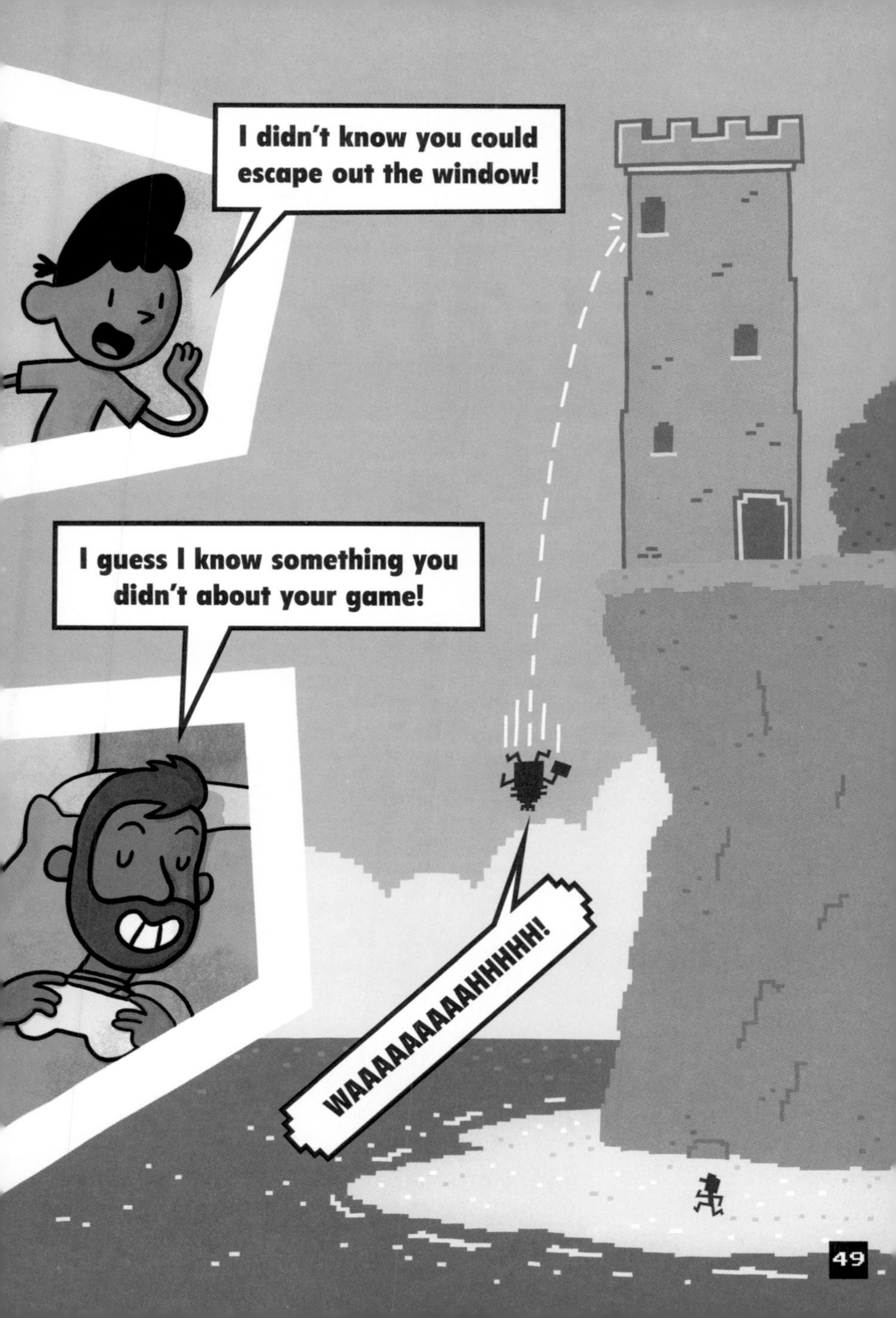
I didn't know you could escape out the window!
I guess I know something you didn't about your game!
WAAAAAAAAAHHHHH!

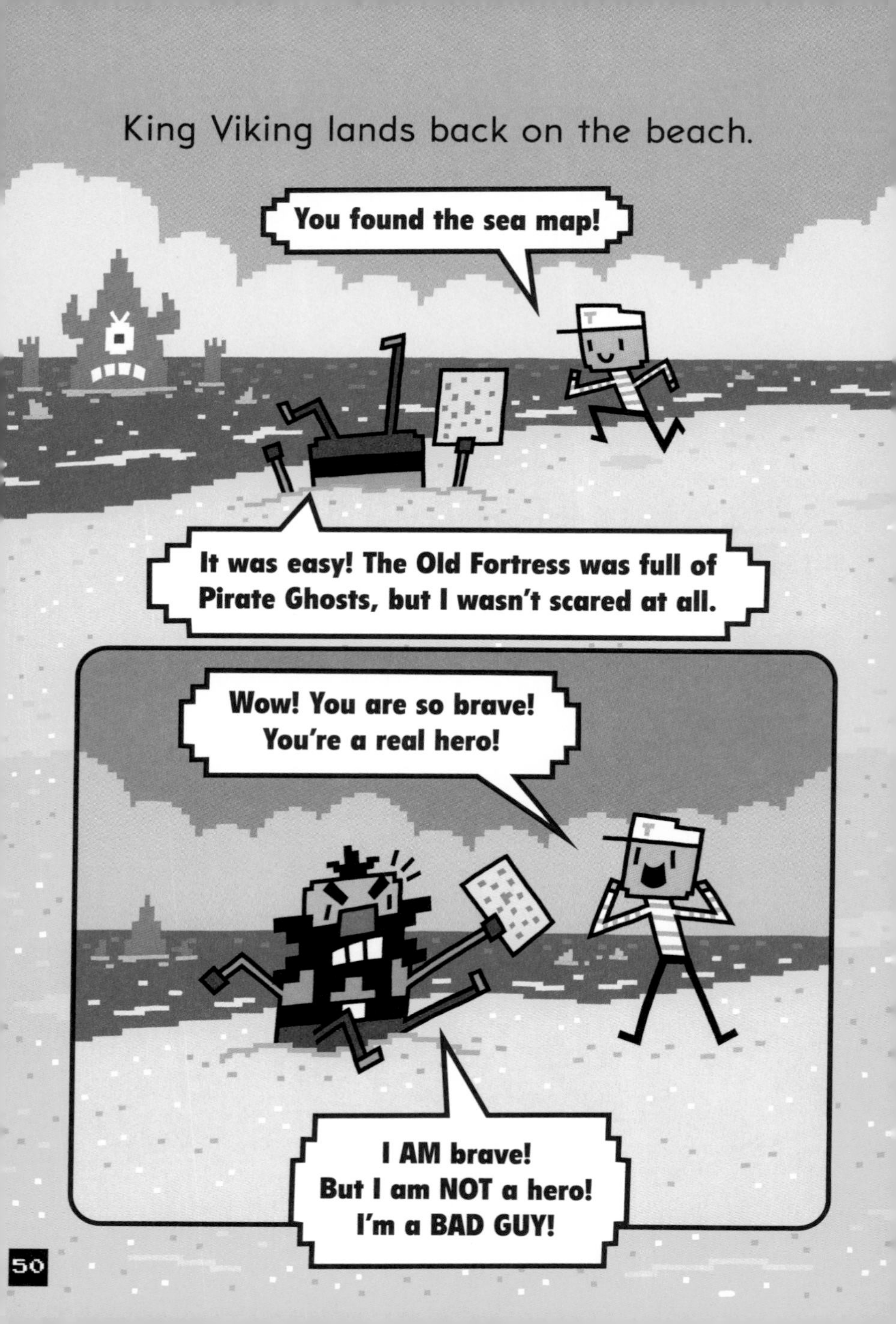
King Viking lands back on the beach.
You found the sea map!
It was easy! The Old Fortress was full of Pirate Ghosts, but I wasn't scared at all.
Wow! You are so brave! You're a real hero!
I AM brave! But I am NOT a hero! I'm a BAD GUY!

8 TROUBLE AT THE TOP

Captain Trevor looks at the sea map.

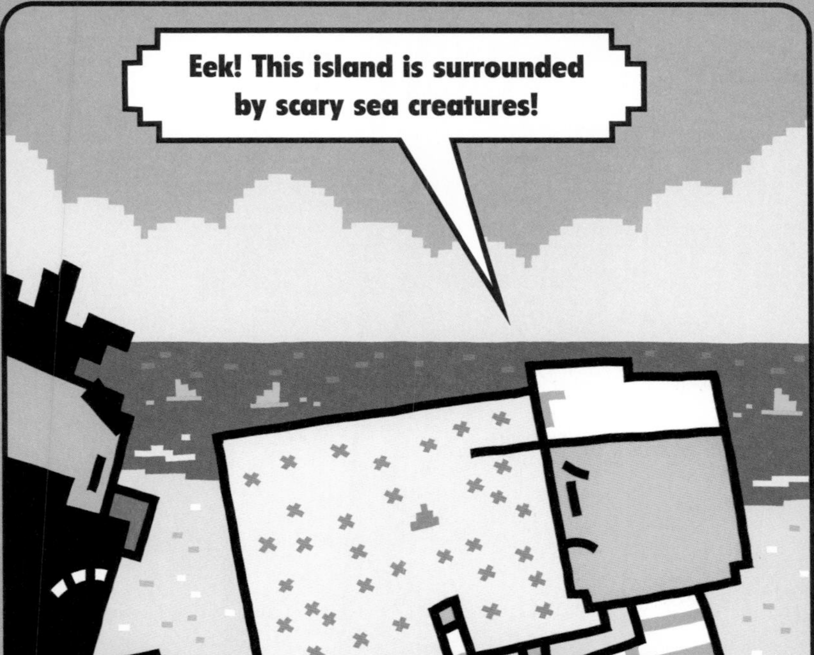
Eek! This island is surrounded by scary sea creatures!

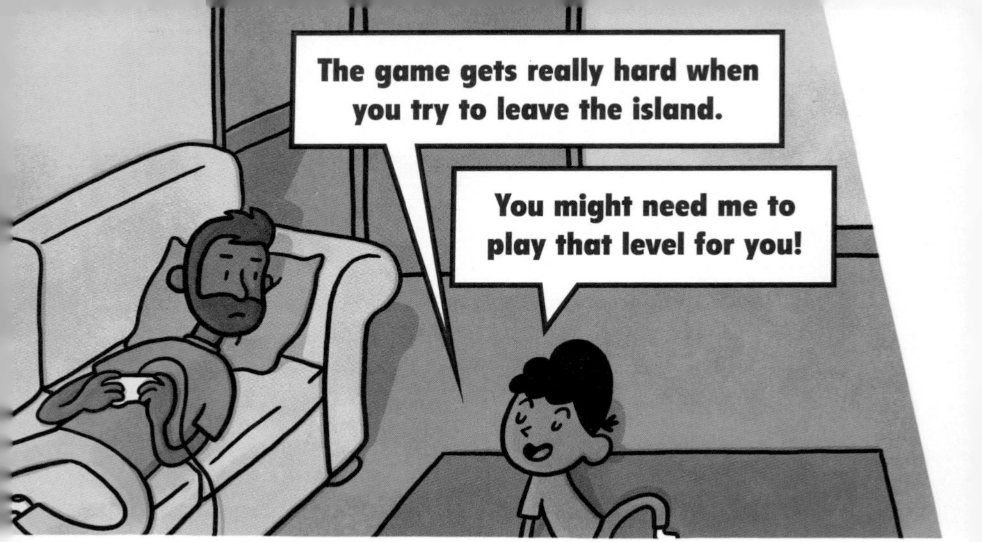
The game gets really hard when you try to leave the island.
You might need me to play that level for you!

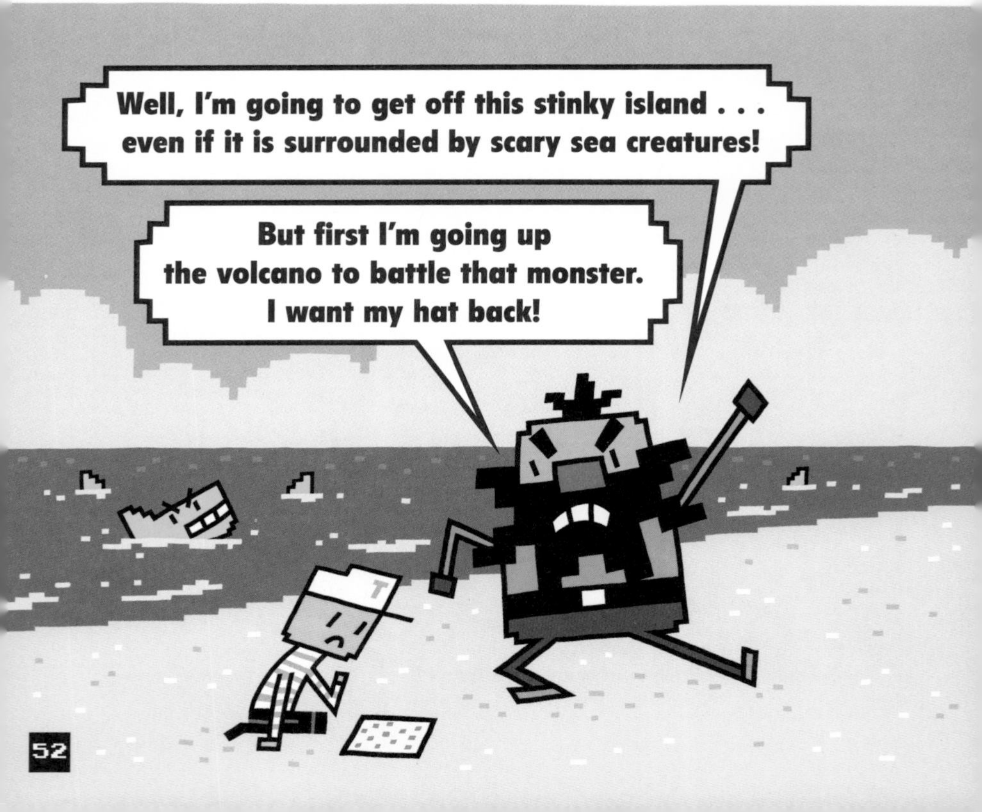
Well, I'm going to get off this stinky island . . . even if it is surrounded by scary sea creatures!
But first I'm going up the volcano to battle that monster. I want my hat back!
T

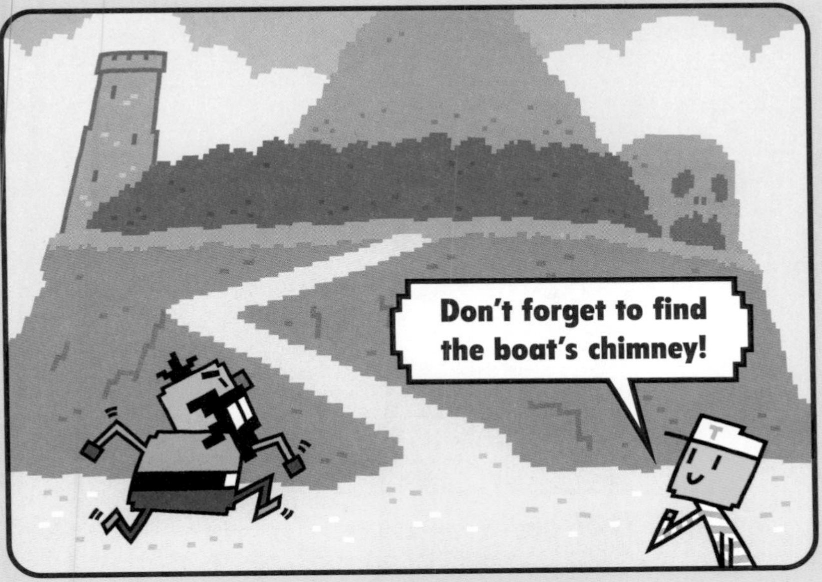
Don't forget to find the boat's chimney!

King Viking starts to climb up the side of the volcano.

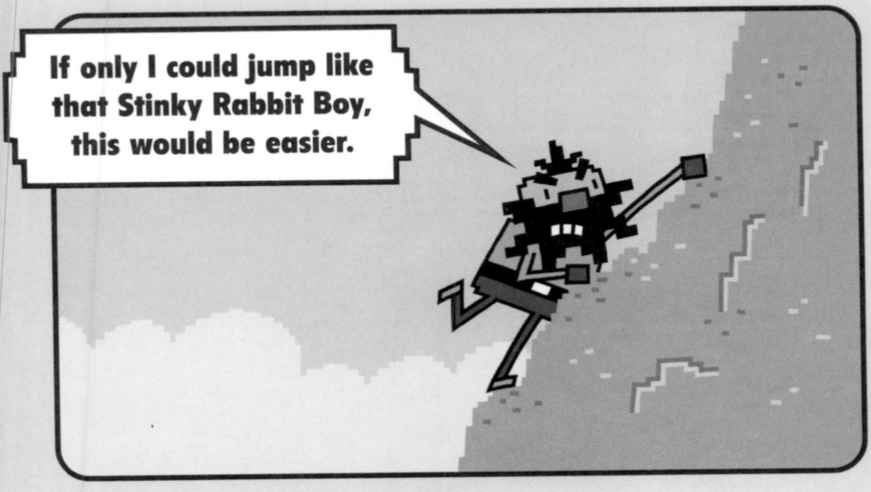
If only I could jump like that Stinky Rabbit Boy, this would be easier.

King Viking keeps slipping and falling. Seagulls swoop down to peck at him.

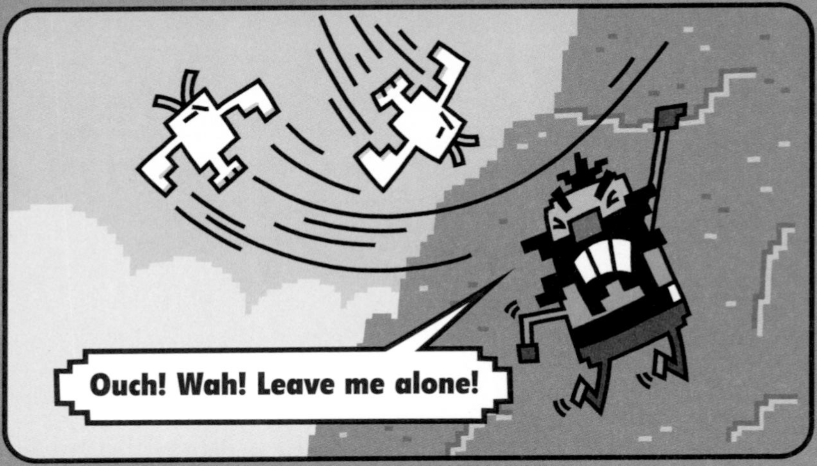
Ouch! Wah! Leave me alone!

He also keeps stopping to collect coins.

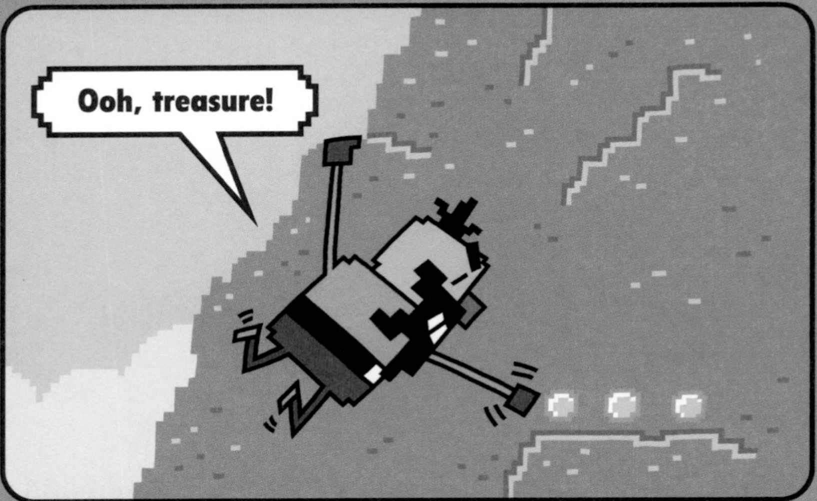
Ooh, treasure!

Finally, King Viking makes it to the top of the volcano.

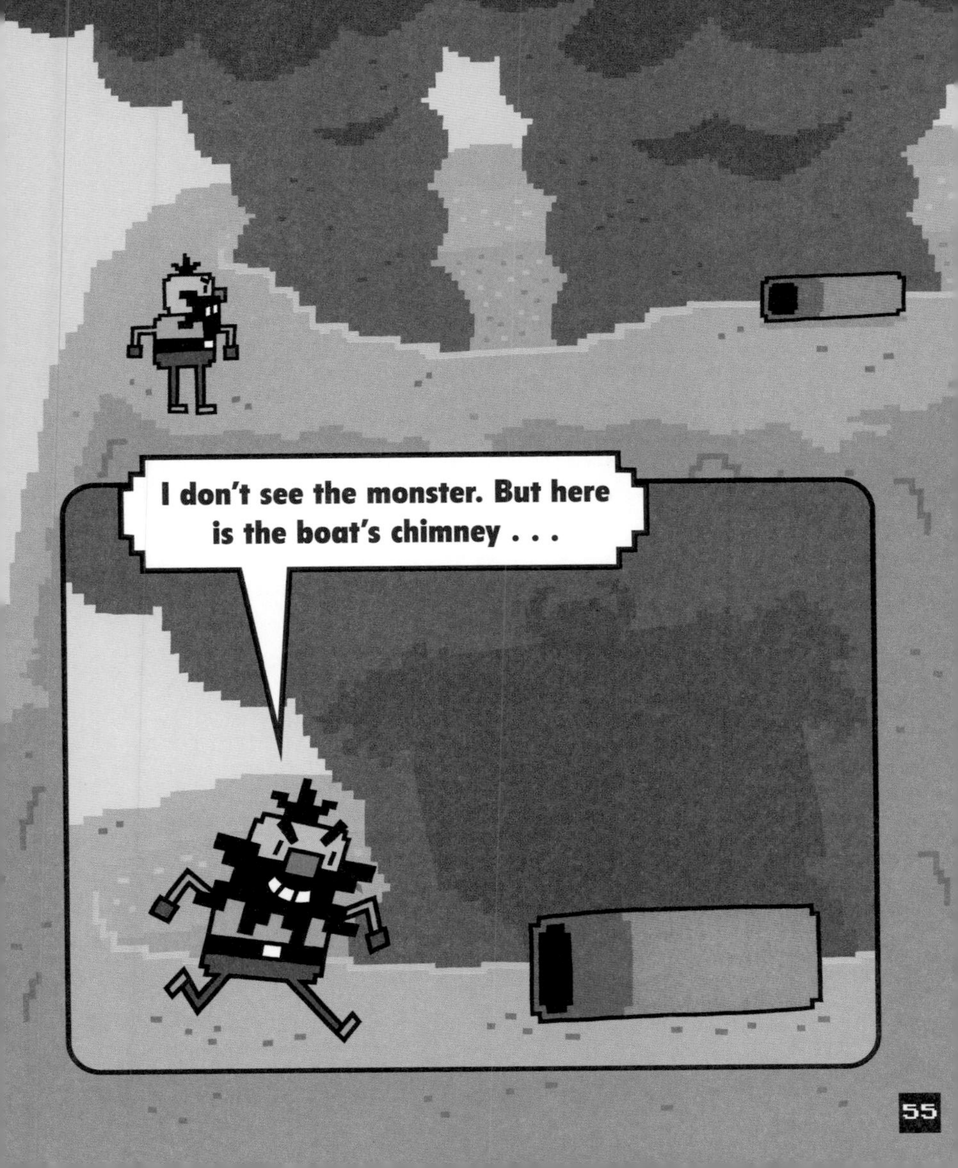
I don't see the monster. But here is the boat's chimney . . .

The monster <u>is</u> here! And it is still wearing King Viking's hat! The monster snatches the chimney.

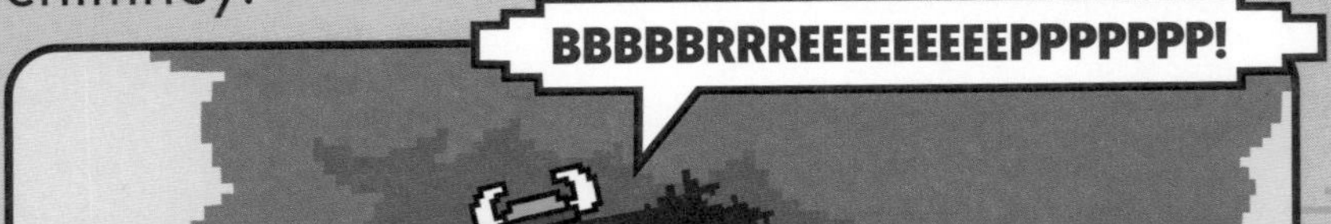
BBBBBRRREEEEEEEEEEPPPPPPP!
Wah!

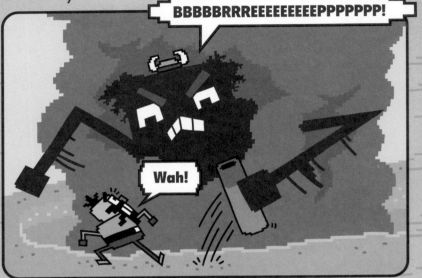

King Viking runs away as fast as he can. The monster runs, too.

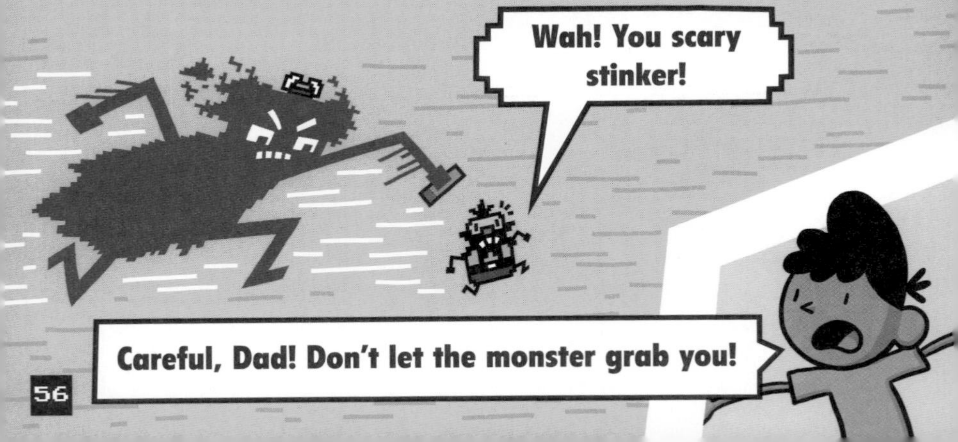
Wah! You scary stinker!
Careful, Dad! Don't let the monster grab you!

THE SECRET
UNDER THE HAT

King Viking is getting tired. He cannot run
any further.

Wait a minute — I am King Viking!
I'm too brave to run away.

King Viking stops running. He turns around to face the monster.

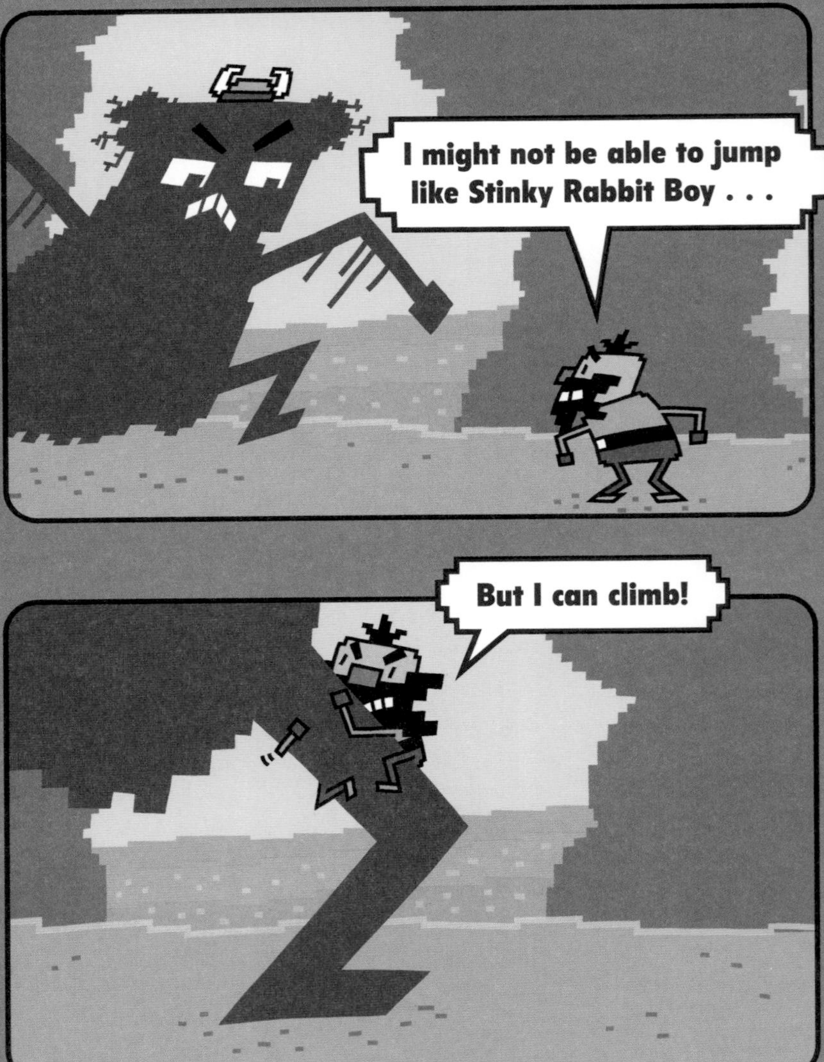
I might not be able to jump like Stinky Rabbit Boy . . .
But I can climb!

King Viking climbs up the monster, all the way to its head.

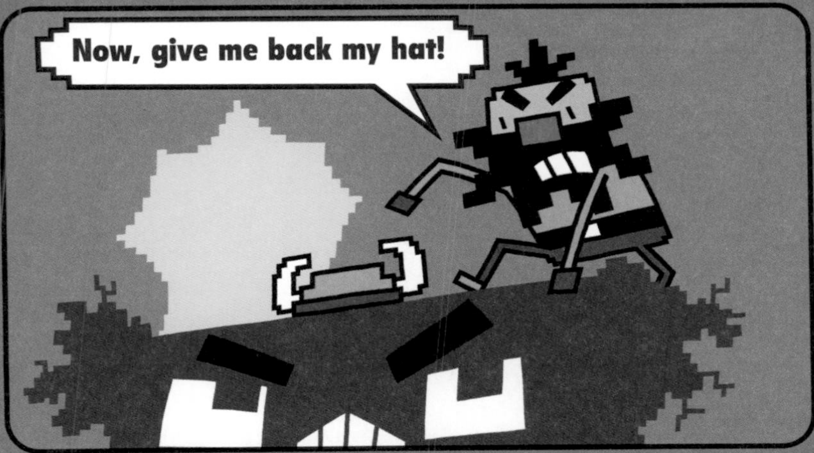
Now, give me back my hat!

King Viking lifts the hat and spots something on top of the monster's head.

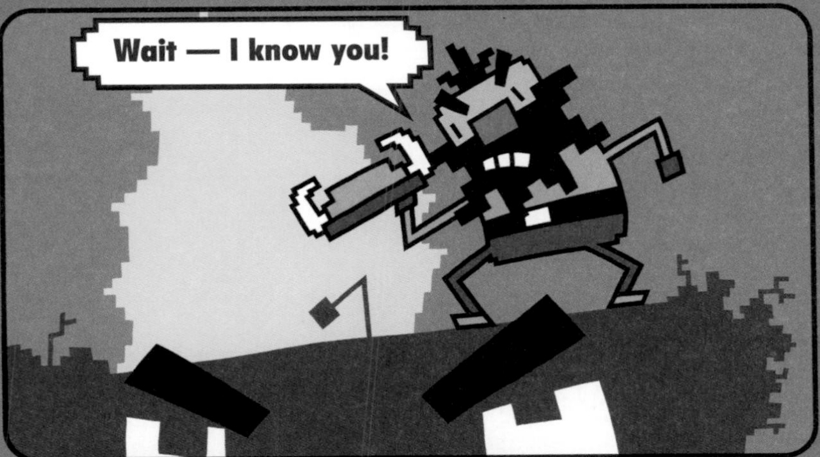
Wait — I know you!

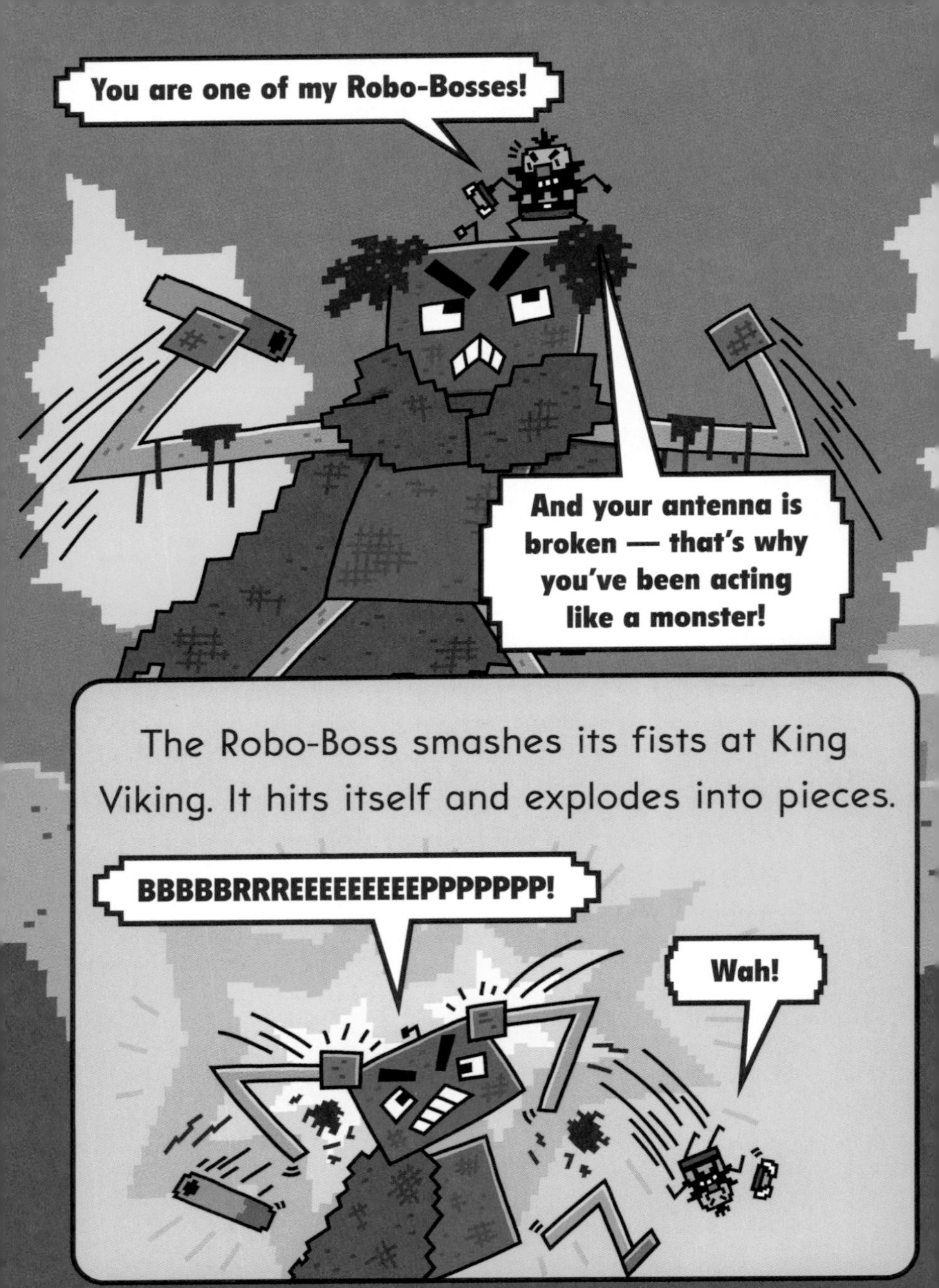
You are one of my Robo-Bosses!
And your antenna is broken — that's why you've been acting like a monster!
The Robo-Boss smashes its fists at King Viking. It hits itself and explodes into pieces.
BBBBBRRREEEEEEEEEEPPPPPPP!
Wah!

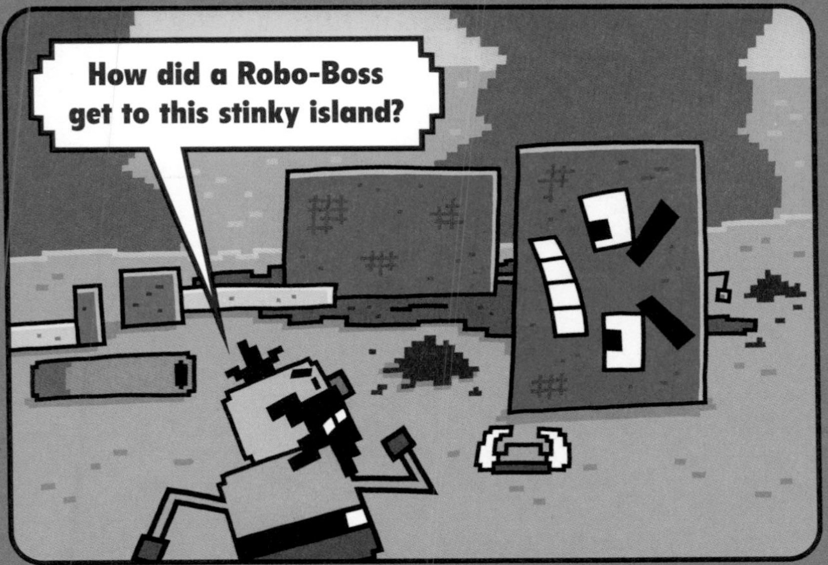
How did a Robo-Boss get to this stinky island?

King Viking quickly fixes the Robo-Boss's broken antenna.

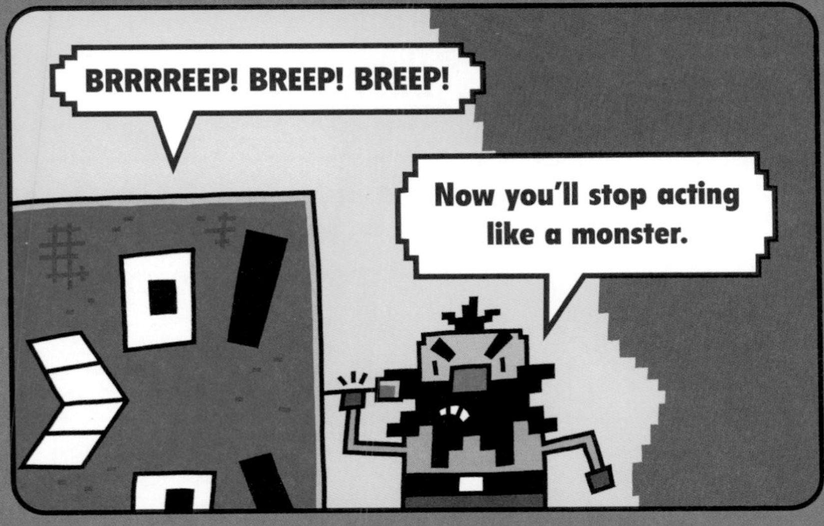
BRRRREEP! BREEP! BREEP!
Now you'll stop acting like a monster.

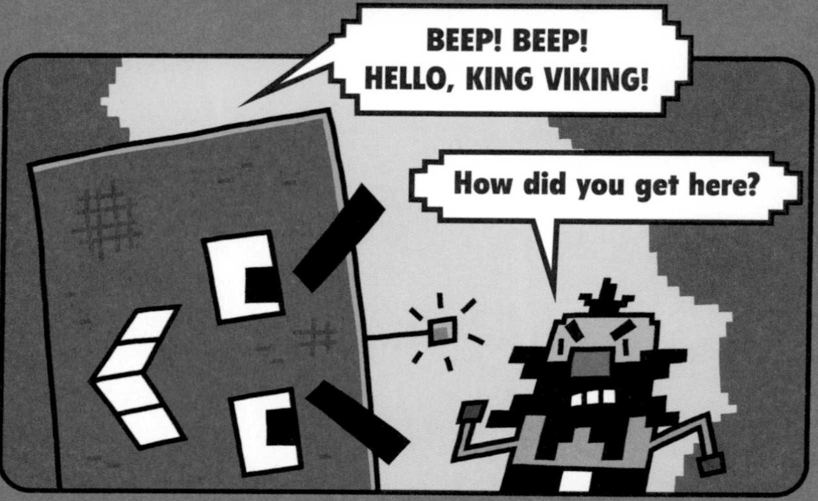
BEEP! BEEP!
HELLO, KING VIKING!
How did you get here?

The Robo-Boss explains. It was sent flying through the air a long time ago when Super Rabbit Boy beat them in battle.

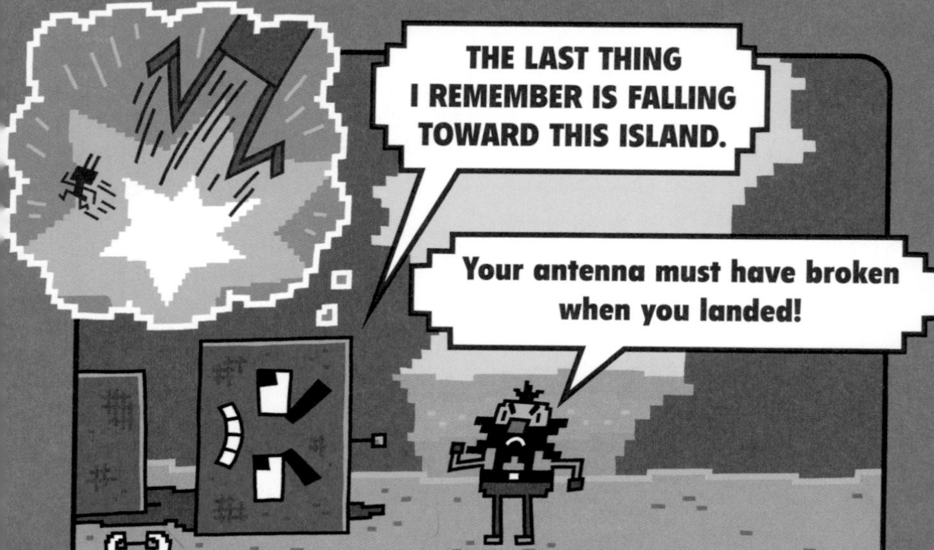
THE LAST THING I REMEMBER IS FALLING TOWARD THIS ISLAND.
Your antenna must have broken when you landed!

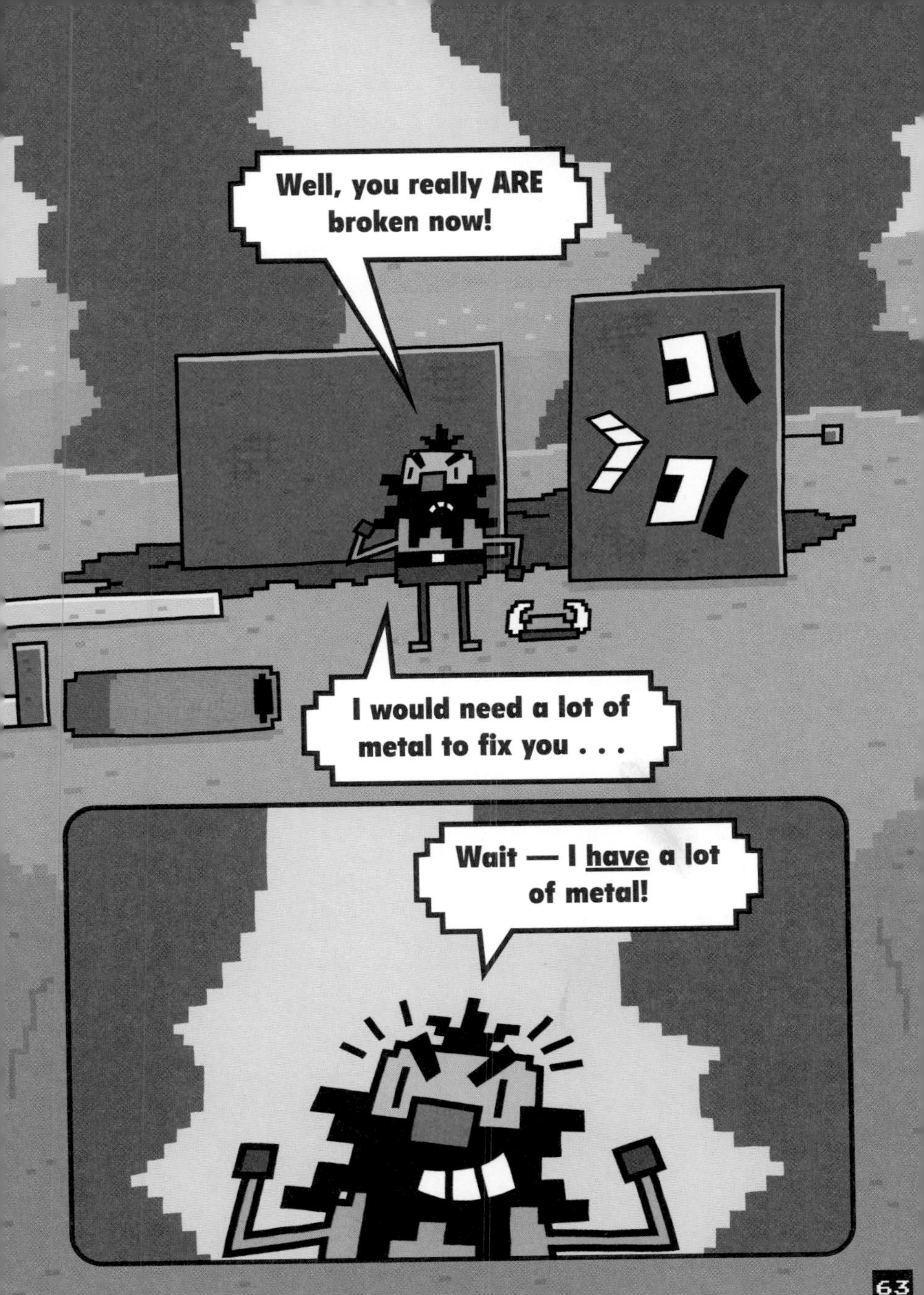
Well, you really ARE broken now!
I would need a lot of metal to fix you . . .
Wait — I have a lot of metal!

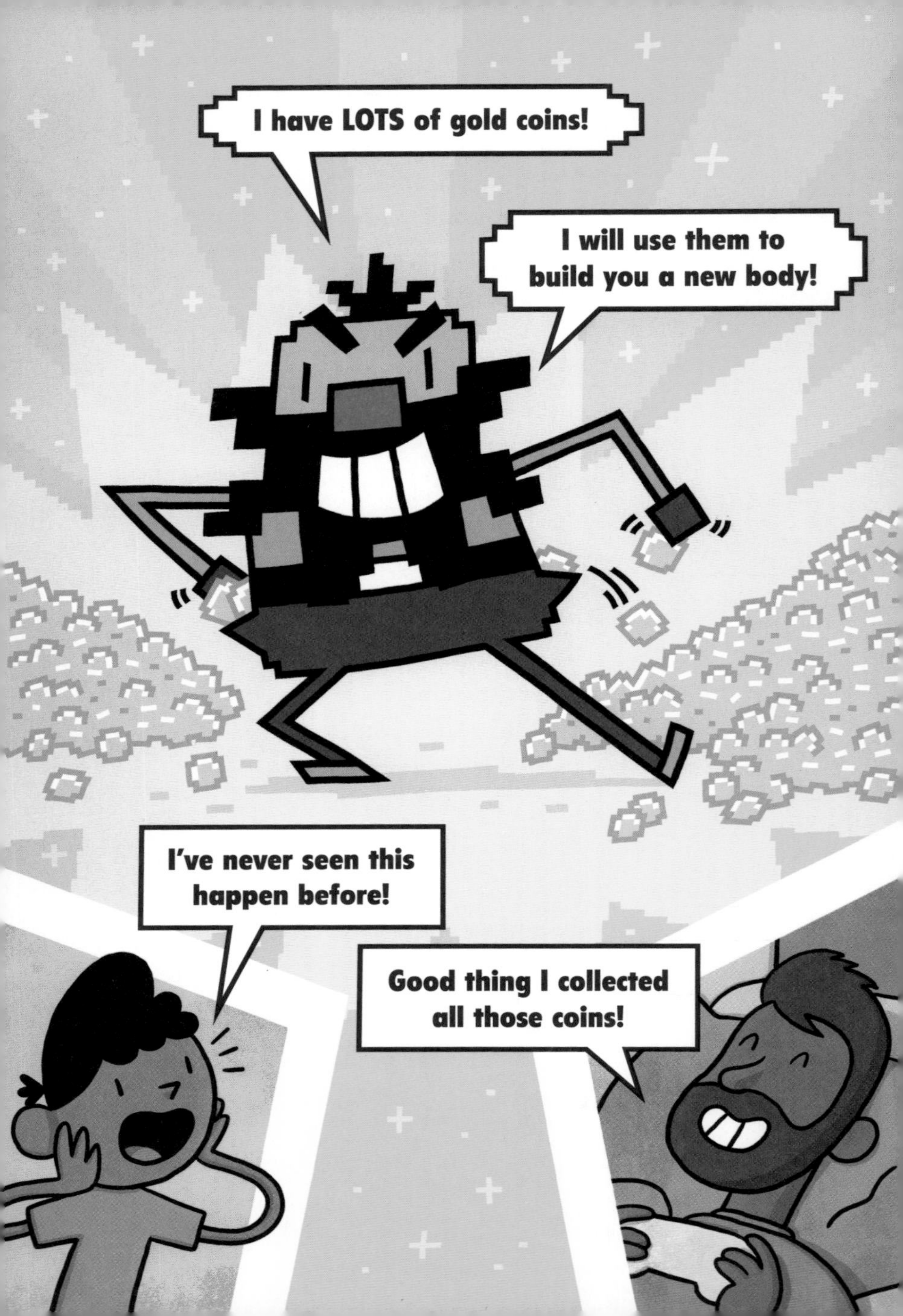
I have LOTS of gold coins!
I will use them to build you a new body!
I've never seen this happen before!
Good thing I collected all those coins!

King Viking and the fixed-up Robo-Boss head back to the beach. Captain Trevor is busy looking at the sea map.

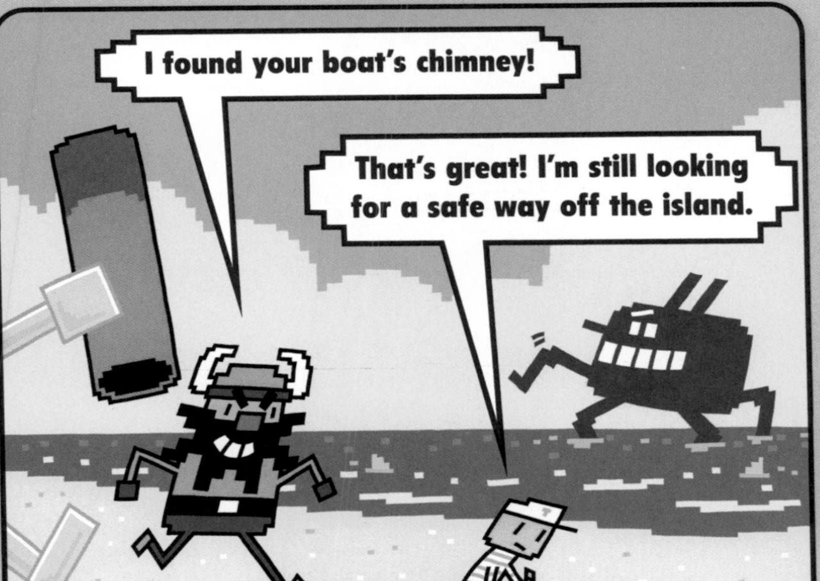
I found your boat's chimney!
That's great! I'm still looking for a safe way off the island.

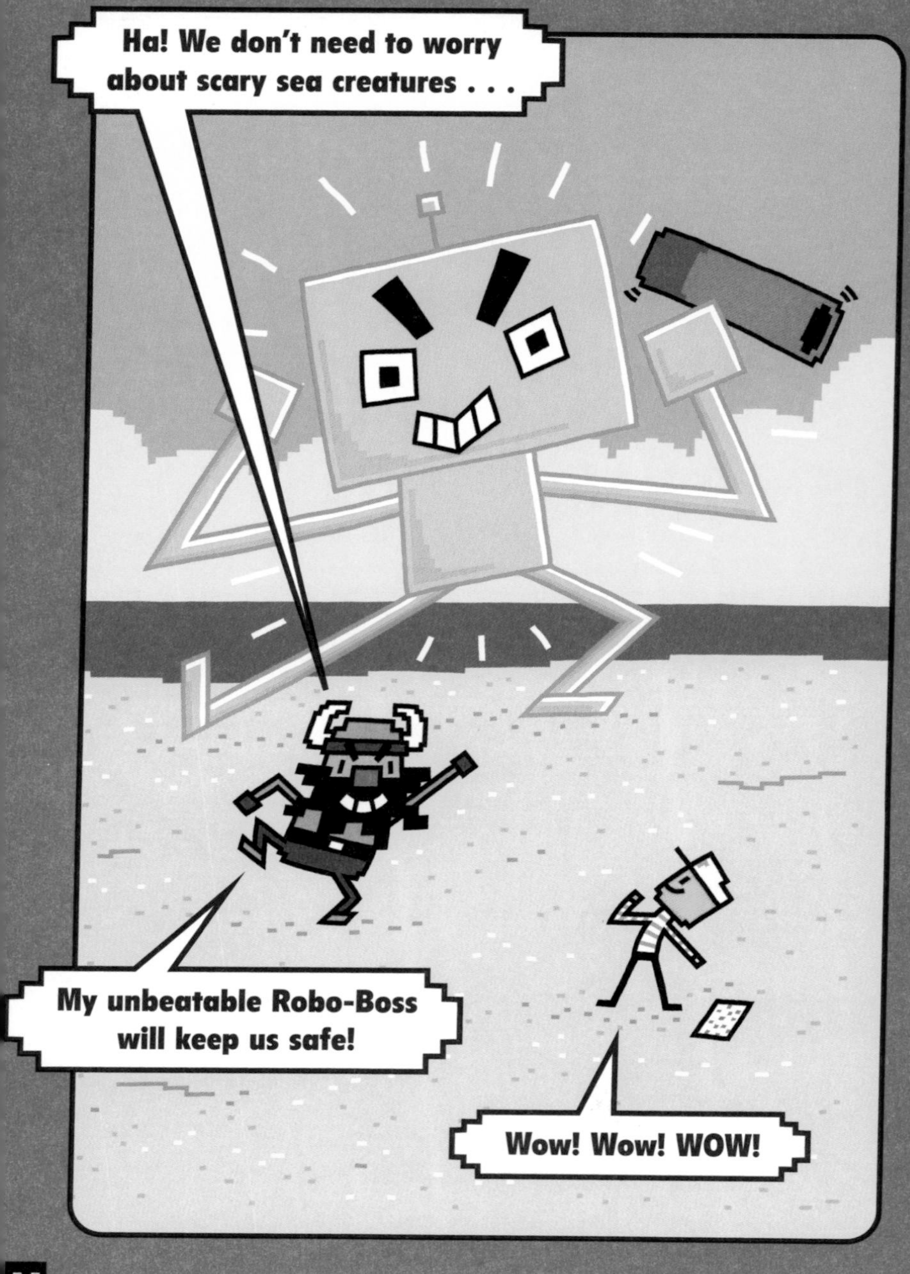
Ha! We don't need to worry about scary sea creatures . . .
My unbeatable Robo-Boss will keep us safe!
Wow! Wow! WOW!

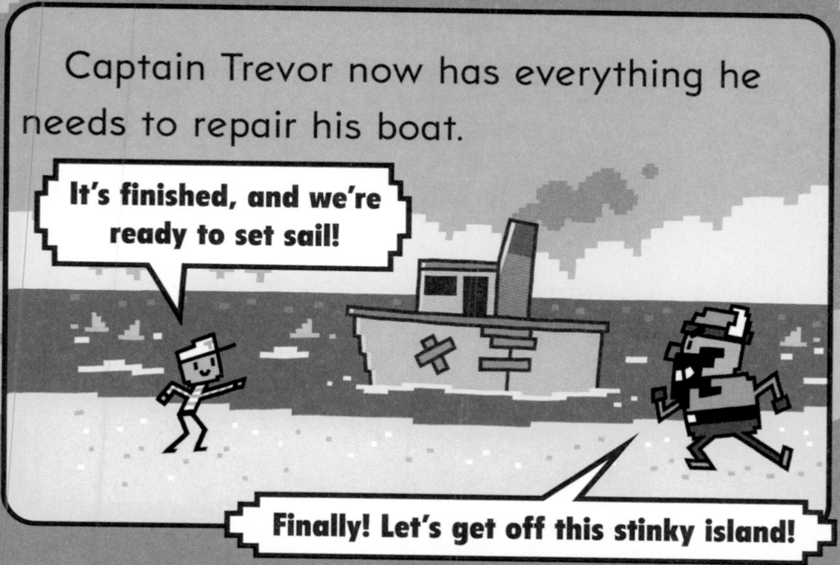
Captain Trevor now has everything he needs to repair his boat.
It's finished, and we're ready to set sail!
Finally! Let's get off this stinky island!

On the Scary Sea, the boat is quickly surrounded by scary sea creatures.

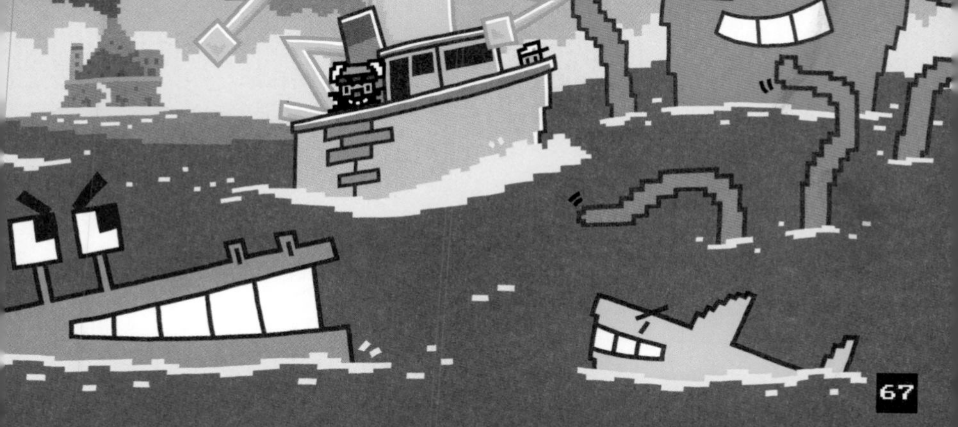

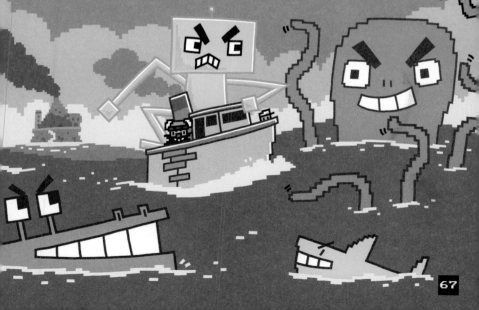

But the Robo-Boss has no trouble keeping the boat safe.

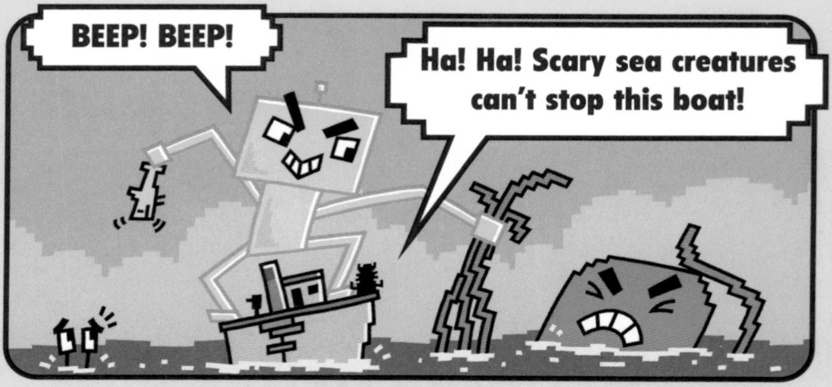
BEEP! BEEP!
Ha! Ha! Scary sea creatures can't stop this boat!

Captain Trevor sails the boat out of the Scary Sea. King Viking is almost home.

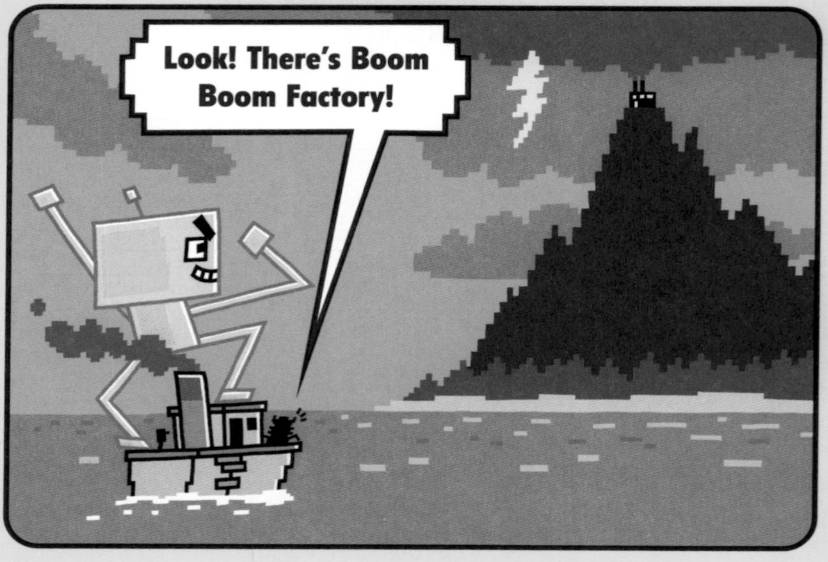
Look! There's Boom Boom Factory!

Captain Trevor leaves King Viking and his Robo-Boss on the mainland.

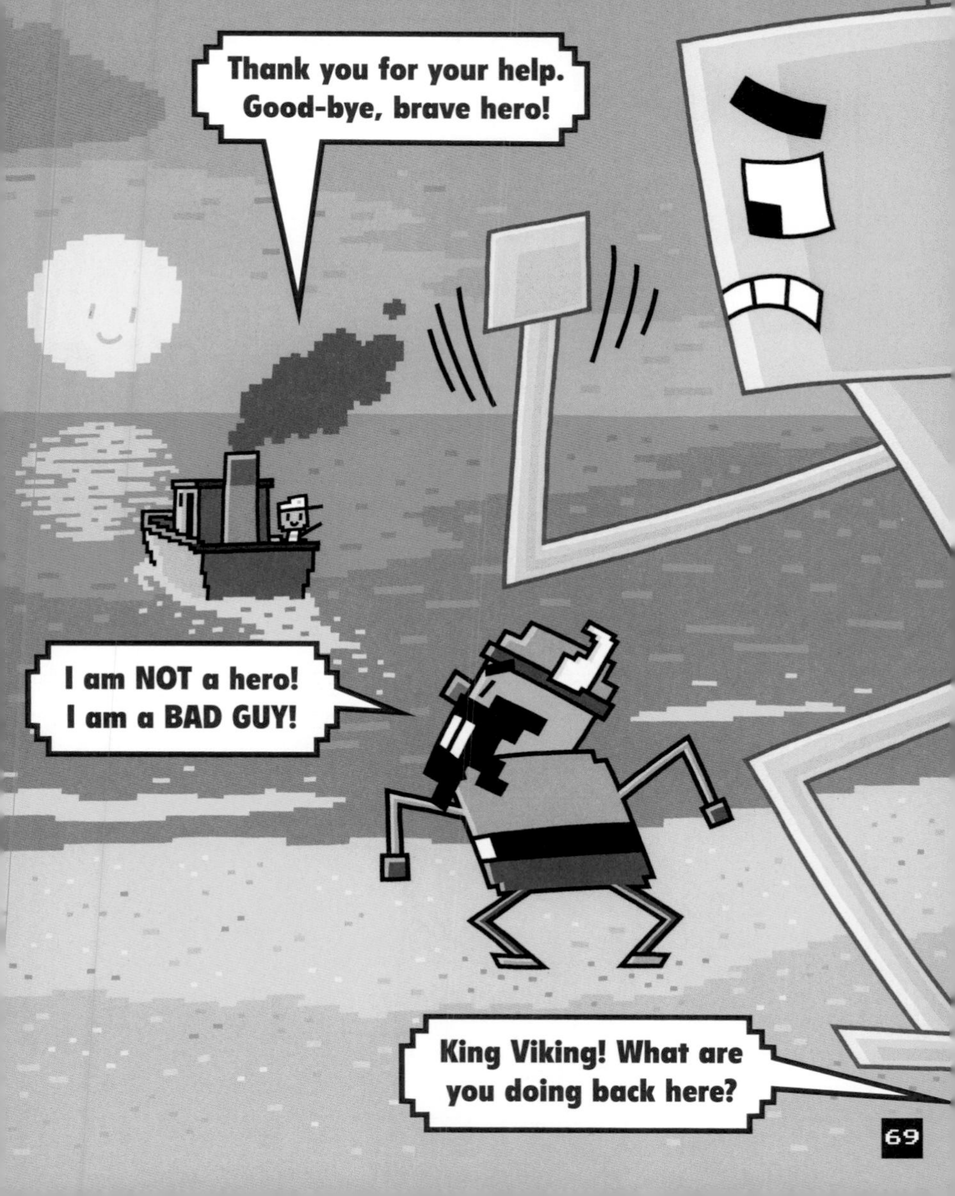

Super Rabbit Boy and the animals are still partying on the beach.

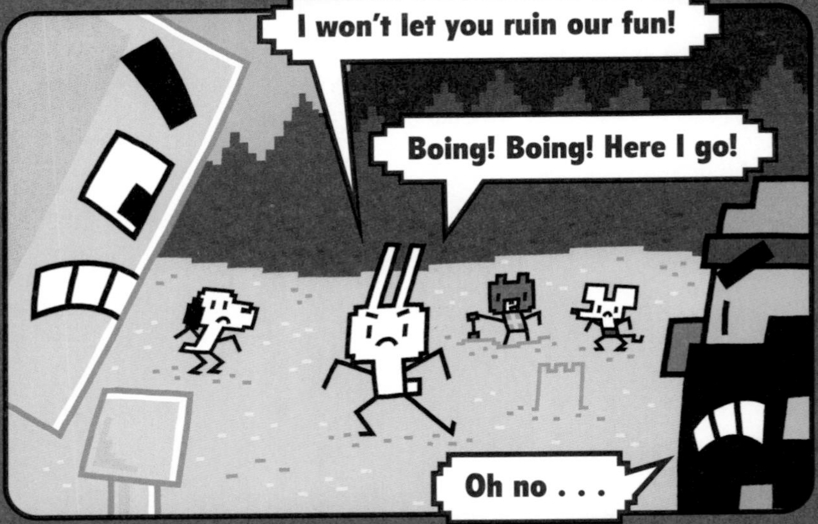
I won't let you ruin our fun!
Boing! Boing! Here I go!
Oh no . . .

Once again, King Viking and the Robo-Boss are sent flying through the sky.

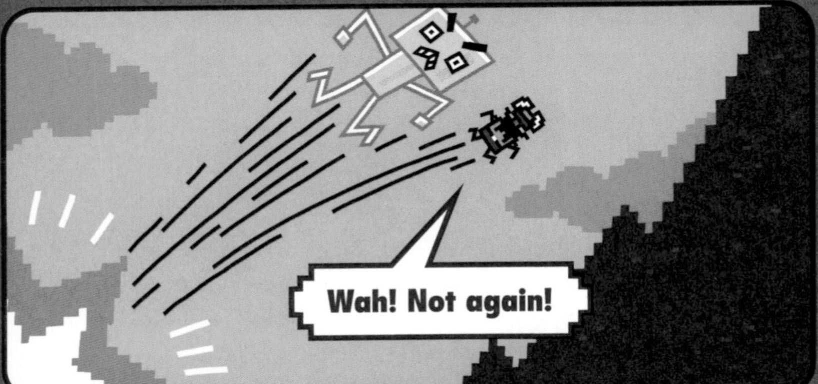
Wah! Not again!

But this time, they crash right through the roof of Boom Boom Factory.

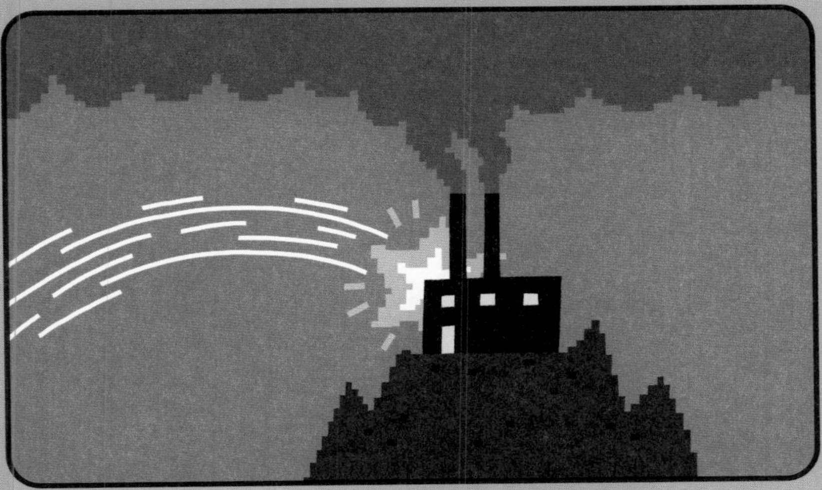

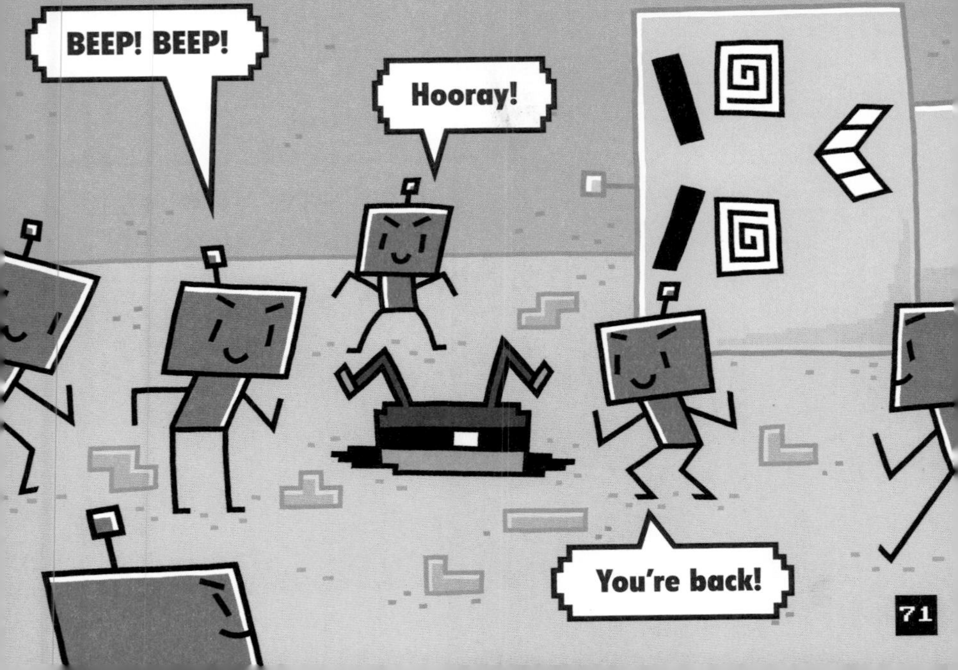
BEEP! BEEP!
Hooray!
You're back!

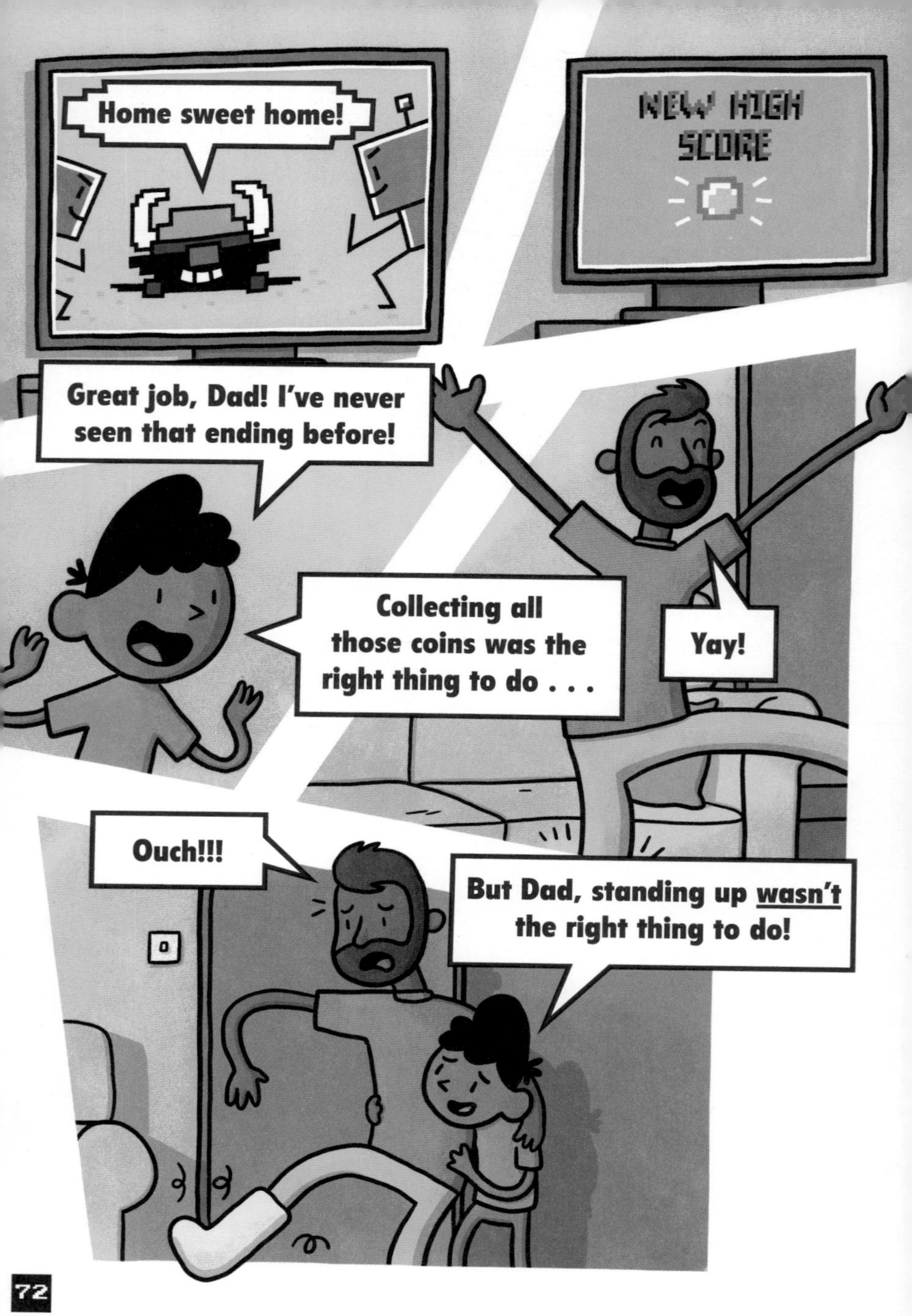
Home sweet home!
NEW HIGH SCORE
Great job, Dad! I've never seen that ending before!
Collecting all those coins was the right thing to do . . .
Yay!
Ouch!!!
But Dad, standing up wasn't the right thing to do!

THOMAS FLINTHAM

has always loved to draw and tell stories, and now that is his job! He grew up in Lincoln, England, and studied illustration in Camberwell, London. He lives by the sea with his dog, Ziggy, in Cornwall.

Thomas is the creator of THOMAS FLINTHAM'S BOOK OF MAZES AND PUZZLES and many other books for kids. PRESS START! is his first early chapter book series.

King Viking has lost his hat again. Can you find it?

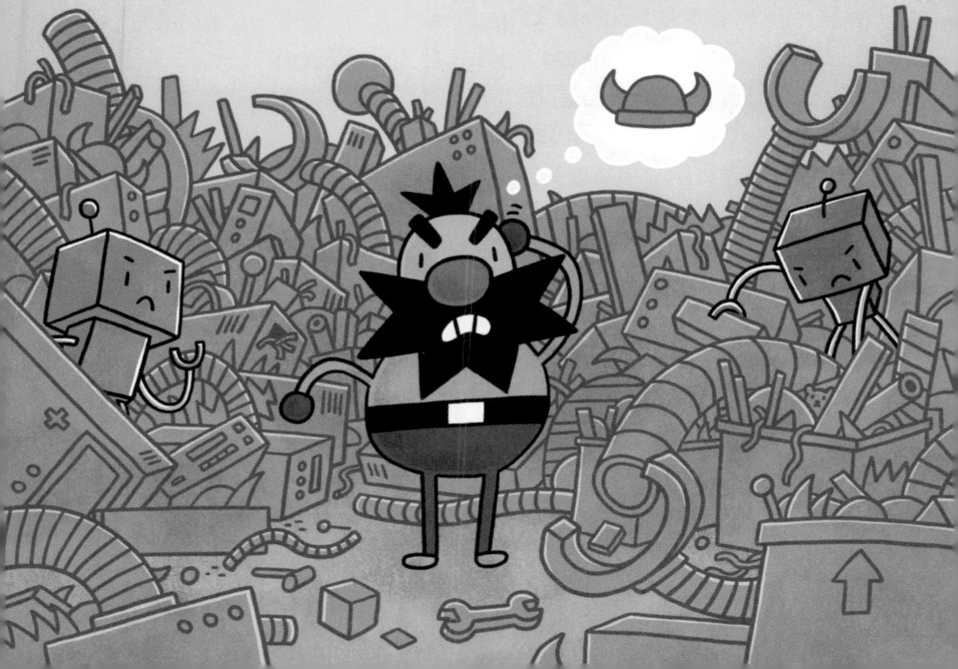

PRESS START!

How much do you know about SUPER KING VIKING LAND!?

What does Sunny's dad — as King Viking — like to collect throughout the game? How does this help him in the end?

King Viking meets Captain Trevor. How did Captain Trevor get to the island? What does King Viking need to do to get them both off the island?

Super Rabbit Boy is usually the hero of these books. But this time, King Viking is the hero! How does he feel about being a hero? Reread pages 21, 50, and 69.

The island's monster turns out to be something surprising. What is the monster REALLY? And how does King Viking help it?

Captain Trevor needs <u>three</u> supplies to fix his boat. Can you name them without looking back? Draw a picture of Captain Trevor fixing his boat. Then label the supplies he uses!

scholastic.com/branches